CHAS WILLIAMSON

Paradise Series: Book One

WHISPERS
in Paradise

Print ISBN: 978-1-949150-71-1

eBook ISBN: 978-1-949150-72-8

Year of the Book

135 Glen Avenue

Glen Rock, PA 17327

Dedication

This book is dedicated to Janet, my love, the special woman who won my heart with just a smile decades ago. You've given me a fairy tale life full of happily-ever-after. Your encouragement and belief in me allowed me to fulfill my dream of writing. If God let me design the perfect woman, it would be you.

Any heroine I create could never match your qualities of kindness, goodness, love, wisdom or inner (and outer) beauty. In other words, you are perfect and I'm very lucky.

Acknowledgments

To God, for creating all types of love, including romantic love. And also for giving me the gift, desire and courage to pursue my dreams.

To my best friend, for everything.

To Demi, publisher extraordinaire, for shaping the raw words into this book.

To my beta readers, Connie, Jackie, Sarah and Janet for their help and guidance.

To everyone who encouraged me as well as to everyone who discouraged me, for your negativity had just the opposite effect. It fueled my resolve.

For all the authors who've come before me. I recently read that one who reads lives a thousand lives. Thank you for taking me places I never would have seen.

The Campbells

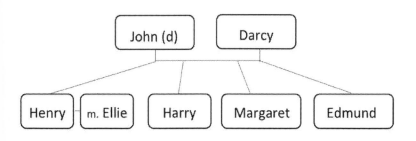

John (d) — Darcy

Henry — m. Ellie — Harry — Margaret — Edmund

The Millers

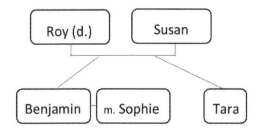

Roy (d.) — Susan

Benjamin — m. Sophie — Tara

Prelude

*E*dmund Campbell stood to the left of his brother Harry, two over from the groom, his other brother Henry. His ribs were sore, a result of the "talking to" he'd received the night before. Sure, he probably shouldn't have been so touchy with his future sister-in-law, Ellie... or her best friend, Sophie. And yes, he should have paid attention when Henry told him to knock it off. But he hadn't, and his torso now carried the black and blue proof from his eldest brother's wrath.

The band was playing the wedding processional. His partner for the evening was a Hawaiian bridesmaid. During the rehearsal, she'd made it clear he'd better keep his hands to himself or she'd give him something to regret.

As the bridesmaids walked down the aisle, he heard Harry draw a quick breath. The man was clearly fixated on Sophie's sister-in-law, Tara. She was kind of cute, but a little too plump for his tastes. Hmm. *What do you see in her, Harry?*

As the evening progressed, Edmund couldn't help but notice the way Harry continued to stare at

1

Tara. His next oldest brother danced with her three times. Harry usually never had much to say—at least verbally—but tonight, his eyes said it all. Harry was hooked.

The rivalry between the two youngest brothers was deeply rooted. When Henry had gone away to war, Harry stepped up as the patriarch of the family. Edmund resented it. *Big old dumb Harry.* Edmund loved showing Harry up. *Why should tonight be any different?*

Edmund waited until the next slow song came on. He walked to Tara, who had just finished dancing with Harry. Edmund's best smile graced his face. "We haven't been formally introduced. I'm Edmund, Henry's youngest brother. Would you do me the honor of allowing me to dance with the prettiest girl here?"

Tara blushed, but her face wasn't nearly as red as Harry's. For a few seconds, Edmund worried Harry might throttle him right then and there.

Her smile was engaging. "I'd be delighted. Name's Tara."

Her hands were soft, but thicker than the other girls he'd danced with. Edmund held her tightly. "So what do you do, Tara?"

"I'm a nurse practitioner. My duties are a lot like a doctor's."

Edmund worked his charms. "Intelligent as well as beautiful. And your voice? So sweet. How can it be that a gem like you hasn't been taken?"

Tara's eyes widened and her face turned a deeper shade of red. She looked away. "Thank you, but I'm not pretty."

"Au contraire. To me, you are the most beautiful woman I've ever met."

Her smile widened. "Really?"

Edmund wrinkled his nose. "Surely. My sister-in-law, the bride, and her friend Sophie are quite fetching, but in no way can their beauty compare to yours."

"Th-thank you."

"Are you seeing anyone?"

Tara looked away. "No. I just recently became certified. My life's been studying and working."

Edmund raised his eyebrows. Out of the corner of his eye, he could see Harry watching like a hawk, fuming over the attention Tara was giving Edmund. "Hmm. Would you mind if I e-mailed you... or better yet, came to visit when I stay with Henry and Ellie? It would mean the world to me."

Her eyes were twinkling. "I-I would love that."

Edmund made sure to keep up his barrage of compliments, even after Harry left the reception early. She was kind of cute, in a homely sort of way. *Bet if I play this right, I can make her fall in love with me.*

Chapter 1

Ashley Snyder wiped her brow and bent over to place her hands on her knees. *Mom was right. Not ready for this.* Her stamina wasn't there, yet. It was three miles to home if she turned around. She'd never make it. A white pickup slowed as it approached.

A man wound down the driver's side window. "You okay?" He had an English accent.

"Might have overestimated my strength. I'm a little wiped."

"Need a ride?"

Fear rose in her throat. *Mom warned me about strangers.* "N-no. I'll be alright."

He shrugged his shoulders. "Suit yourself." The stranger wound up the window.

The world started spinning. The gravel along the berm bit into Ashley's knees as she fell. The man was suddenly beside her, lifting her in his strong arms as if she were a pillow.

"Take you to Ellie. She'll help."

"No. I'm okay, really."

"Nonsense."

Before she could protest, he strapped her in the passenger seat, then uncapped and thrust a cold bottle of water into her hand.

"Drink."

Oh God! He's so big. Suppose he attacks me?

The man executed a three-point turn and sped down the road. In less than two minutes, he pulled into a parking lot. A strange looking building sat next to the pavement. The construction looked new. A barn-like structure with a storefront stared back at her. A second pickup and a sport utility were parked out front. Next to the door, a beautifully decorated hand painted sign sat, not yet mounted. It read, 'Essence of Tuscany – Tea Room and Olive Oil Emporium'.

The man ripped open the passenger door, unlatched her seatbelt and again hoisted her effortlessly. His smell was fragrant, like flowers and so intriguing. He swiftly carried her into the building. Inside the door, an old Sonny and Cher song played over speakers. Two women's voices were drowning out the original artists.

The man yelled over the noise. "Girl needs help." The music stopped. He gently sat her on a cushioned couch. His eyes searched hers. *Concern?* "Found her on the road. Almost fainted."

Two women were there quickly. A short, beautiful blonde and an attractive black-haired, pregnant woman knelt beside her.

The blonde also had an English accent. "Did you hit her with the lorry, ya big oaf?"

The man's face turned red. Ashley studied his profile. Brownish red hair. Very muscular. Handsome, but rugged face. *Did I mention handsome?* "No. Drove past. Looked like she needed help."

"I'm fine, really. Just got a little dizzy, that's all."

The black-haired girl brushed Ashley's long tresses from her face. She was also quite pretty. "Can I get you anything? I'm Ellie Campbell. This is my best friend, Sophie, and my brother-in-law, Harry. How can we help you?"

Ashley's pulse was slowing down. *He only wanted to help me, not hurt me.* "I'm Ashley Snyder. I-I live a couple miles from here. Just out for a walk, though I guess it was too much. I've been pretty sick lately, but thought I felt strong enough to go for a hike."

The man's voice was softer. "Need food?"

Ashley shook her head.

The blonde held her hand. "It's unusually warm today. Maybe the heat got to you." She turned to the man. "Make yourself useful and get a cold cloth."

The one they called Harry shot Sophie a mean look, but headed to another room. He returned almost immediately with a wet towel. Sophie reached for it, but he turned his shoulder and gave it to the black-haired girl instead. Ashley almost laughed out loud.

Ellie shook her head and giggled. Her eyes were large and brown. When she smiled, dimples were evident in her chin and right cheek. She gently wiped Ashley's face with the cool cloth. "Relax. You're among friends now."

The blonde, Sophie, held her hands. "Is there someone you want us to call?"

Mom! She'd be so mad. Her mother had forbidden Ashley from leaving the house. *Gotta get home, now!* Ashley pushed Ellie away.

"I-I've got to leave. Mom will be home at six. Have to be there before she arrives. If I start walking..."

Sophie stroked her hair. "How far away do you live?"

"Three, maybe four miles."

"Huh, funny we've never seen you around. Lived here three years."

Sophie's perfume smelled like daffodils. "Can't be late. Mom'll kill me."

Harry stood before her. So tall. So confident. "Nobody'll hurt you. Promise you that. I'll take you home, then." He knelt and patted her hand. "Need to eat. We'll call out."

"I, uh, don't have any money."

His eyes were kind. Sparkly brown. Harry winked at her. "My treat."

***

Ellie saw the exchange. The reaction on Ashley's face when her eyes engaged Harry's was easily read. The girl liked him, really liked him. *Good. Harry needs someone.* Her brother-in-law didn't fool her. There was so much more to him than he allowed anyone to see. So devoted to his family. Always the first out the door and the last in at night, that's how he paid them back. Harry's way of showing love.

Ashley's eyes followed him as he closed the door behind him. "Nice guy, isn't he?"

8

Ellie poured her a glass of tea. "That he is. You said you were sick. Care to talk about it?"

Ashley studied her glass. "I had cancer and beat it. Not once, but twice." For the next half hour, she told Sophie and Ellie all about it. How she nearly died the first time. They'd caught it early the second go 'round. She'd been homeschooled all of her life. Ashley pawed at her eyes. "Dad died two years ago, a heart attack. Mom's always taken care of me, but it's been tough on her." She bit her lip. "Never had a lot of friends. Who wants to hang with the sick girl?"

Sophie let out a sob and wrapped her arms around Ashley. "We do. You've made two good friends today."

A male voice echoed the sentiment. "Three." Ellie watched Ashley's face light up when Harry returned. He set the food down and gave her a bear hug.

Ashley seemed reluctant to let go of Harry. After she did, the girl quickly wiped her cheeks. "You people are so nice. Wish I could see you guys every day."

Ellie took in the young girl's pale appearance, her thick and unruly blonde hair. Poor child. No friends, until now. *This is what we're about, helping others.* Ellie patted Ashley's hand. "We can arrange that."

***

Tara Miller placed her glasses on the desk so she could massage her temples. She loved taking care of people, but the paperwork was a killer. Her last patient left the treatment room before seven, but she'd be stuck in the office until at least ten. Not only did she have patient notes to write (*why did they do away with dictation?*), but there were continuing education credits to complete. She glanced across her desk at the framed photo of Edmund.

Tara's heart warmed as she thought of him. She remembered well the day they'd met. At the wedding of his brother Henry Campbell and the beautiful Ellie Lucia. She'd liked Henry, a lot, from the day she met him. Such a gentleman.

A text alert on her phone beckoned. From Edmund.

Miss you. Call when you leave. I'll be waiting.

Edmund and his brother Harry had been at the wedding. She'd been attracted to both, but for different reasons. Where Edmund was gregarious and outgoing, Harry had such a depth about him that made her heart beat fast. He didn't say much, but his eyes and hands betrayed him. Harry had been attracted to her at the wedding. His big, tough hands trembled when he held her while they danced. And his eyes...

A second message.

I'll ice the wine.

Tara had also danced with Edmund. She remembered how his words affected her, despite having to fend off his roaming hands. Tara smiled. Edmund sure did love to touch her and that touch drove her wild. Two days after the wedding, he started e-mailing her, five times a day. His messages were funny and romantic, although he couldn't spell very well. The attention he doled out to her made her weak inside.

Tara again glanced at his photo. Their first trip to the beach. Early on, Edmund had begun Skyping her weekly. Within a month of his first e-mail, he confessed his love for her. By then, Tara had realized she was also in love. He came to America twice that year, at Christmas and at Valentine's Day. Tara blushed as she remembered what they'd done the first night he arrived.

"Thank you, God, for sending Edmund." Studying had never come easy for her. She'd spent so many hours concentrating on learning her profession, she was sure life and love had passed her by. But that was before Edmund rocked her world. *The love of my life.* She kissed his photo and then put her glasses back on so she could attack her stack of charts. She hoped she'd have enough energy for Edmund when she got home. He certainly would.

***

A few miles away, Susan Miller, Ben and Tara's mother, sat down to have an evening cup of tea. The nights were the worst time for her since her husband had passed on. Life was lonely. True, Ben and Tara lived within walking distance and made efforts to include her in everything, but she tried to respect their time with the ones they loved.

Ben had never been happier in his life. His marriage to Sophie appeared perfect, though she wondered when they would give her grandchildren. She'd joked with them about it until recently. The last time she'd broached the subject, Sophie started to cry and left the room. Sophie always seemed to be crying, but Susan had picked up bitterness in her tears that evening. She hadn't brought up the subject since.

Her thoughts drifted to her own daughter. Tara appeared to be in love with that Scotsman, Edmund. She suspected they slept together, but Tara was a big girl. Maybe someday soon they'd get married and have children. Edmund was nice, but a little too touchy in public when it came to Tara. While Edmund treated Susan like royalty, his roving eye every time a pretty girl was around upset her. She hoped he wouldn't break her little girl's heart.

Looking out the window, she noted how brightly the home of Ellie and Henry Campbell was lit. Henry had brought his brothers and mother to live with them shortly after the wedding. *Now talk about a couple in love!* They were great neighbors, always looking out for her. Ellie took the time to visit a couple of times a week. Susan smiled as she thought of her neighbors. Ellie called Susan her 'Mummy', which was what Sophie called her. *Yes, I'm blessed.* It was like having three daughters. Life was funny, with the little turns and quirks.

Susan took a sip of her jasmine flavored tea. Sophie had explained that Ben and Ellie had once been lovers. The fact that they were now neighbors and such close friends was indeed strange. *Would I have been a grandmother by now if Ben married Ellie?* She realized she was being selfish. Sophie was wonderful and Susan was grateful for Sophie's presence in the family.

Her mind once again drifted back to Sophie and the last time she'd brought up starting a family. Susan hoped and prayed something wasn't wrong, something that might affect their ability to have children. The bitterness in Sophie's tears that night had been heart wrenching for Susan. Like she'd pulled a scab off a nasty wound. *I hope it was only my imagination.*

Chapter 2

*O*n the brightly lit house just across the road from Susan Miller's, Harry carried the carton to his room. He fondly thought of poor Ashley. So pretty and dainty, like a china doll. She touched him in a way he'd never felt before. Ellie had shared Ashley's story after he dropped the girl off at her home. He knew Ashley liked him a lot, but Harry's heart belonged to another. Only time would heal that wound.

The smell of roast lamb still lingered in the house. Harry slipped off his work clothes before sprawling on the bed. He was tired. Though a man of few words, he hoped Henry and Ellie knew how much he appreciated them inviting him to live with them here in America. He missed Scotland, but not as much as he'd feared. A man with very few friends, family was everything to him. Now that they were all together, he felt complete. *Almost.* His sister Margaret was living in State College where she was a sophomore at Penn State University. She was working on a double major in Agricultural Science and Business Management. Her goal was to run the farm she had purchased, the one that bordered Ellie and Henry's property.

Harry smiled as he thought of Margaret. His baby sister was his closest friend. Today was Tuesday. Harry made it a point to visit her every Wednesday. True, she'd be home Friday afternoon for the weekend, but he was faithful in his weekly visits. Margaret was the only one to know his secret, who he really was. He called her cell.

A chipper Scottish voice answered on the first ring. "Harry! How's my older brother?"

He smiled, glad to hear her voice. "I'm well, Maggot." That had been his father's pet name for her. "Want a visitor tomorrow?"

"Yes, I'd absolutely love that. I miss everyone, but especially you. Class runs until eleven. Shall we do our normal? Meet me at my apartment, say around eleven-fifteen? We'll go out for lunch."

"Delightful. Need anything?"

"Well, if Mum has any leftovers she wants to get rid of, that would be great. How's the baby doing?"

Harry smiled as he thought of the life growing in Ellie's belly. "Mother and child are fine. Ellie's tired. Help out when I can. Henry and I, one of us is always with her. Starting to show. Think she'll go early."

"It's great to know someone's there for her. I was so excited to find out we'll have a niece to spoil."

"Me, too. Subject change. Package came today."

Harry had to pull the cell away when Margaret shrieked. "Is it what I think it is?"

"Yep."

"When can I see it?"

"Tomorrow. As always..."

She laughed. "I know, I know. It's all a big secret."

They talked for a few more minutes before saying goodbye. Harry opened the box, removing the book with the glossy cover. He paged through before locking it in the big storage trunk in his room. Only Margaret knew what was in that trunk. The family had speculated about its contents, but he kept it secret. Edmund brashly told everyone that was where Harry kept his stash of pornographic magazines and dirty movies. He never acknowledged or denied his brother's allegations, but it wasn't what Edmund thought. Harry found pornography revolting. *Women are something special, to be placed on a pedestal and honored, not lusted over.* If his family knew the contents of the trunk, they'd fall over in shock.

***

The raindrops were cold as Tara stepped from the car. Edmund appeared with an umbrella and wrapped his arm around her. Tara was excited. It had been a long time since she'd been inside the Fulton Theater in downtown Lancaster. If it hadn't been for the rain, the concert would have been held at the amphitheater at Long's Park.

The scowl on Edmund's face matched the feelings he expressed about going to the event. "We can find something else to do instead of seeing a silly old concert. Maybe spend the afternoon in your hot tub, sipping on wine. In fact, we could, you know..." He sent a suggestive wink her way. "Like you promised."

Tara kissed his cheek. "I did, but we agreed to come to this event first. I've never seen Ellie play. Sophie says she's really good."

He let out a sigh. "Of course Sophie would say that about Ellie. My sister-in-law is her best friend."

"Yes, and both are like sisters to me. I don't understand why you never want to have anything to do with your family. Why is that?"

He mumbled something under his breath and closed the umbrella. "Since you're an Ellie fan, let's sit down front."

She touched his arm. "No. I want to sit with the family. Sophie promised to save us seats." Tara led him to the row where Ellie's family sat. Edmund hesitated. She squeezed his hand. "After you."

Edmund kissed the cheeks of his mother and sister, Margaret. But when he passed Harry, he viciously pinched his brother's arm. Harry responded with a quick punch to Edmund's leg. Edmund limped past. Tara laughed and shook her head. *You deserved that, Edmund.* She patted Harry's hand as she scooted down the row as well. Edmund continued beyond his other brother Henry, then past Ben and Sophie. He left an open seat for Tara next to Sophie.

Sophie hugged her. "Missed you, Tara. Even though we're neighbors, I don't get to see you enough. Edmund keeps you from us too often."

"I agree. Maybe you and I can do brunch tomorrow?" Sophie nodded.

Tara turned to Edmund, who was rubbing his leg. "You okay?"

"That stupid brother of mine punched me. Gave me a Charlie horse. You see that?"

"He hit you after you pinched his arm. Quit acting like a child."

"He deserved it."

Tara lowered her voice. "Why do you hate Harry? He's a very nice man."

"*Humph*. You don't know him. Always been mean to me."

Before she could say anything else, the house lights dimmed and the curtain opened. Ellie sat with her trumpet in her lap. She waved at her family.

"Ladies and gentlemen," the director announced, "it seems the weather brought us inside the Fulton this afternoon. Thank you for joining the Lancaster County Jazz Ensemble for our spring concert. We hope you enjoy the show."

Tara smiled and listened as the band played song after song, many of which featured Ellie on her trumpet. When it was over, Henry ran up, kissed his wife and presented her with a bouquet of flowers. Henry turned to Tara and Edmund. "I'm taking Ellie out to celebrate. Everyone's coming. Will you join us?"

Edmund shook his head. "I'm pretty tired. We'll pass this time." Tara could see the disappointment in Henry's face.

Tara grabbed his arm. "I want to go."

Edmund gave her his come-on smile. "We did what you wanted, now about your promise..."

Anger rose up inside her. *Is that all you care about?* "Thought you were so tired? If you're too tired to go eat supper with your family, then we're not going to risk your safety in the hot tub."

He winked. "I'm never too tired for that."

She turned to face him. "I'm hungry and I want to go out... with our family. Don't want to go? Fine. I'll catch a ride home with my brother. See you tomorrow."

His face turned red. "Tara..."

That got your attention. She stared him down. "Take it or leave it. We can do the hot tub after dinner or skip it tonight. Your choice." His mouth dropped open. Tara turned to her brother, Ben. "Edmund's tired, but I'll come. Can you drop me off at home?"

Ben started to reply, but Edmund interrupted him. "Changed my mind. We're both coming."

In the car, Tara turned to Edmund. "What is it with you and your brothers? Don't you realize how blessed you are to have your family here?"

"They're not as nice as you think." He reached for her hand.

Tara pulled away from him. "Tell me what you mean."

He grabbed her hand. "They're mean to me."

She again slipped from his grasp. "If you can't talk to me, don't touch me."

The look he shot her was pure anger. "Does that mean just now, or later as well?"

"Both. Now explain yourself. Why don't you like them?"

They rode in silence for a few minutes before he spoke. "You don't understand what it was like. Henry's a big war hero with all his medals, the pride of the family. And when he joined the service, Harry took his place as the head of the household and resident darling. Margaret and Mum always treated him like he was something special, but me, not so much."

What Edmund didn't know was that Ellie and Margaret had filled in some of the blanks about the feud. "Would that have anything to do with you being lazy, especially when it came to chores?"

Edmund's mouth dropped open. "Me? Lazy? Who in the world told you that?"

I have an older brother, too. Tara touched his arm. "I can imagine what it was like, being the youngest. I've seen first-hand how hard of a worker Harry is, how devoted he is to the family. And Henry. Wow! Ellie was lucky to get him."

Edmund almost swerved off the road. "I see. They're wonderful and I'm nothing. I know you like Harry. Maybe you should be with him instead of worthless old me. Figures. Those two always get everything."

Tara brushed his hair but he pushed her hand away. Tara reached over and kissed his cheek. "No, they don't. You didn't let me finish. I'm the one that got the pick of the litter." His lips were pursed tightly together. "I love you, Edmund, but I really want you to try and be nicer to your brothers. When you and I get married, we're going to live next to them."

His voice was tinged with anger. "Who said anything about marriage?"

The cold sensation of disappointment ran down her arms. Tara leaned against the door and looked out the window.

Edmund must have realized he'd crossed the line. "Didn't mean that. Of course we'll get married, someday."

She wiped the moisture from her eyes. "I'm beginning to doubt that."

Edmund pulled the car to the shoulder. Tara turned to him. "What are you doing? We'll be late for the meal."

He touched her face. "I know where they're headed, we'll catch up in a jiffy. I'm sorry, Tara. I love you. You know that, don't you?"

Her heart still stung from his comment. "You love *me*? Or just love what we do?"

Edmund squirmed in his seat. His eyes didn't meet hers. "Not what we do. I love you."

"Really? Enough to prove it? Maybe we'll stop the hot tub and everything else for a while. Now what do you have to say, smart mouth?"

He swallowed hard. "If that's what you want."

She saw right through him. "What I want? You don't have a clue what I want. I'm just a fun time for you." She turned away.

He gently grasped her chin and turned her face to his. Tara's vision was blurry and she wiped her eyes. "What you want is love... and commitment."

She smacked his hand and stared through the windshield. "Like I'll ever get either from you."

Once again, he turned her head to face him. "You will get it, soon. I promise." He wiped her tears away. "I know I'm immature at times, but never doubt how I feel about you. You're the love of my life." He kissed her nose. "Bear with me, just a little longer, okay?"

"Why should I believe you?"

"My words seem hollow, but let my actions show it. We don't need to do anything for a while. It's you I love, not the naughtiness."

"Forgive me for not believing, but you've said it before."

His smile was wearing down her resistance. "I have, but this time I'll prove it. Instead of the hot tub, maybe we'll take a long walk in the rain."

Tara started to look away.

"I'll prove it to you. Trust me."

***

Ben watched as Sophie removed her pearls, placing them in her jewelry box. She slipped the red dress from her creamy white shoulders. *So beautiful, so perfect.* The scent of daffodils filled the room. After she slipped her nightie over her head, she turned. Ben was there, waiting, and wrapped his arms around her waist. He knew what was coming.

"Do you know I love you?"

Sophie sobbed and buried her head on his shoulder. "I love you, too."

"It's okay. I'm here."

Ten minutes passed before she could speak. "This is intolerable. I do love Ellie, but this is torture."

Ben had to bite his lips. *Because of me.* "I'm sorry, Soph. This is all my fault."

Sophie shoved him away. "Quit saying that."

"All because I can't..."

"Get it through your thick skull! This was God's choice, not something you did."

He sat on the bed and rubbed his hands over his face. *Please, not another argument.* "We have options. There are thousands of children that would love to have you as a mother."

His beautiful wife stood before him, tears on her cheeks, fists wrapped tightly in anger. "I *do not* want to adopt a child. Can't you understand? I want to carry *our* child."

There it was. The runaway train had just left the station. "Not my child. I can't father children and..."

"You know how I feel. I want to be a mother, to give birth and..."

"Have some other man's kid."

"Damn you. You're so pig headed." Sophie grabbed her pillow and headed for the door. "When you're done wallowing in self-pity, come get me. I'll be on the sofa." The slamming of the door said it all.

Chapter 3

*A*s the weeks passed by, Ashley grew ever fonder of Harry. His hands seemed to tremble on the rare occasions he touched her. For the first time in her life, she felt alive, really living life. Sophie and Ellie seemed genuinely happy to have her with them.

One Monday morning, both women arrived at her house. *What?* They never both picked her up at the same time.

"This is a surprise."

Ellie was driving. She smiled at Ashley in the mirror. "That's because we're going on a trip. Ever been to King of Prussia?"

"Uh no. Where's that?"

Sophie answered. "Close to Philly. We're picking out teapot covers today. Then we were thinking we'd do a spot of shopping. And there's this divine hibachi place we want to go to for lunch."

"Will Harry be there?"

Ashley caught the look the girls shared. Ellie answered, "Not today. He and Henry had to go to Baltimore. If you don't want to go..."

"No, no. I, uh, just got used to seeing him. He's funny." *And I really, really like him.*

Sophie turned and gave her a crazed look. "Yeah, he's funny alright. Looks a little..."

Ellie laughed and cut her off. "Hey now. That's my brother-in-law you're making fun of."

Ashley looked out the window. *And the man I want.*

The morning was enjoyable. Ashley was surprised when they insisted she decide which pot covers to order. And she'd never been to a hibachi. The food was great and Ashley loved being part of the trio, but she missed Harry, terribly. She'd been thinking about him all weekend and really wanted to see him.

The trip tired her out and Ashley fell asleep on the way home. When the car stopped moving, she opened her eyes. They were parked at the tea house. A quick glance at the dashboard clock brought her heart to her throat. *Look at the time.* Her mom would soon get off work.

"I, uh, need to get home. Can you drop me off there?"

Ellie pulled the keys from the ignition. "Sorry. We're under strict orders to drop you off here."

Panic rose in her throat. "But I'll be late. Who gave you the order?"

"Look out your window."

Harry was standing there with the biggest grin she'd ever seen.

***

Tara couldn't help but smile. *What a wonderful change.* Edmund had been the perfect gentleman for the past two weeks. The way he held her hand and talked with her turned her on immensely. She knew he was doing things he didn't like to do. *For me.* On Sunday, he'd even brought her to Henry's house to have dinner with the family... and for the first time she could remember, he had been civil to both of his brothers. Then last night, he'd surprised her. When she arrived home, Edmund had steaks ready on the grill, but the big excitement had been the company he'd invited over – Ben, Sophie and her mother.

The scent of pulled pork greeted her as he held the car door open. *What a treat!* Edmund knew she loved visiting Roots Market in East Petersburg, but never came along because his family had a stand there.

His smile made her knees weak as he opened the door. "My lady, I offer you the bounty of the land."

Tara wasn't sure her feet touched the ground as he led her to the auction barn. "Why are we in here?"

Edmund stood in line to get a number for the auction. "Because you told me you wanted to plant flowers. I thought we'd buy tonight and plant them tomorrow."

Tara held his hand as they surveyed the choices. Pansies, with purple and yellow faces, caught her eye as did the orange and yellow Shasta daisies. Within a few minutes, three flats of each sat in front of them. Edmund won the bid on two Lilac bushes that were in bloom. One was white and the other purple.

She laughed. "We better stop or we'll be planting all week."

After depositing the flowers in the car, they strolled back to the fruit and vegetable stands. The biggest produce booth belonged to Ellie and Henry's enterprise. Edmund nodded to the boy on the other side of the table. "Tara, this is my friend Sam Espenshade. Sam, the love of my life, Tara Miller."

Love of his life? Tara's hand trembled as Edmund held hers. Soon, Thompson grapes and local strawberries filled the basket he carried. "Anything else you want, my lady?"

Tara searched his eyes. "Yes. Let's get a bottle of wine and some cheese."

Edmund nodded and turned away. She touched his arm. Edmund smiled at her. "It's for tonight. My hot tub is feeling a little left out."

Edmund kissed her nose. "Great idea, I heard there's a meteor shower tonight. I'd like to wrap my arms around you and watch the beauty of the show. Heaven's fireworks, just for you."

Tara couldn't help herself. She kissed him, right in the middle of the crowd. "You won't have to look to the sky for fireworks tonight."

***

Harry was waiting for Margaret when she walked from the building. She jumped in his truck and gave him a hug. "How's my favorite brother?"

"Good. Really, really good."

Margaret studied him. "There's something that's changed about you. You're almost glowing."

Harry blushed. "No, I'm not."

"I'm your favorite sister, right?"

Harry nodded. "Even if I had fifty, you'd still be number one."

"Something you want to tell me? Did you get another package?"

His hands were warm when he gripped hers. "No. Something better." Margaret noticed the blush on his cheeks. He hesitated. "I've met someone."

Margaret's heart leapt. She knew of his heartbreak. Knew how despite his tough façade, he was gentle and tender inside. *Must be the girl Ellie told me about.* "Would it be a cute little blonde lady?"

His mouth dropped open. "How do you know?"

"Ellie told me all about her. So, what's her name?"

The look of joy on his face made her spirit soar. "Ashley. Ashley Lynette Snyder. I think she likes me."

Margaret laughed. "So I've heard. When do I get to meet her?"

"Ellie's aunts are coming to visit next month and Ellie's throwing a little party. I want Ashley to meet the family, but I really want her to meet you. To see what you think of her."

She brushed his hair from his eyes. She'd never seen him so happy. "You're finally over her, aren't you?"

He looked away. "Yes. Finally. Don't want to talk or think about her anymore. Margaret, I think I'm in..." He was breathing hard.

"Love?"

Her tough brother's eyes were glistening. "Yes."

***

Ashley was ecstatic. While Sophie or Ellie picked her up on the days her mother worked, Harry always took her home, every day except Wednesday. He had a standing appointment, but wouldn't tell her with who or where he went. She worried sometimes he had a girlfriend. *Please don't have someone else out there. Want a girlfriend? Open your eyes. Pick me.*

Sophie's shop was almost ready to open. Ashley helped where she could and was rewarded daily with lunch. Her favorite time of day, because Harry always made sure he was there, except Wednesdays, of course.

He was so strong and kind. Harry didn't say much, but he treated her like she was something special. He'd come to know her tastes and always brought exactly what she wanted to eat at lunch. She couldn't help but be attracted to him. *Is it more than just liking him?*

Ashley's thoughts were interrupted when the door to the tea room opened. Harry and another man entered. The man was thinner than Harry, but Ashley could easily tell they were brothers. He walked straight to her. Ashley noted the nervousness in Harry's face. The man's smile seemed genuine.

"You must be Ashley. Ellie's told me so much about you. It's an honor to finally meet you. I'm Henry Campbell, Ellie's lesser half." He gently kissed her fingertips. Ashley felt her cheeks blush. She stole a quick glance at Harry. He was smiling approvingly. *Harry's introducing me to his family.* Her heart started beating wildly.

Ellie's laugh was contagious. "Lesser half, my foot. He's my prince." She reached for and gave her husband a long kiss.

"*Ahem.*" Sophie stood behind him. "Does the handmaiden get a kiss, too?" Ashley stared in disbelief when Henry grabbed Sophie and gave her a kiss on the lips. *What in the world?*

Ellie touched Ashley's shoulder. Ellie was all smiles. Her conversation was directed at Ashley. "Strange, aren't they? Acting like that. Let me explain, Sophie and Henry are the oldest of friends."

"My best friend," Sophie beamed.

Henry took Ellie's hand. "My second best friend."

Sophie blushed. "I meant after my husband, Ben, and Ellie of course."

Harry suddenly cleared his throat. He looked at Henry. "Ask her?"

Henry turned to his brother. "No, why don't you? It was your idea, after all."

Harry's face suddenly turned bright red. "You should. Asked you to."

Ashley was thoroughly confused. "Ask who what? Me?"

Harry nodded, then backed away.

Ellie laughed. "Come on, Harry. We talked about this last night. You should be the one to ask Ashley."

Ashley studied Harry's face. It was turning dark red. "Can't... not in front of... them." His eyes pleaded as much as his words. "Pick you up early? Tell you then, okay?"

She didn't know which caused the butterflies in her stomach... the pleading eyes, him picking her up early or how adorable he was. "When will you stop by?"

"Two hours early. Need to show you something and to ask..." He seemed embarrassed and the laughter coming from Sophie and Henry didn't help him.

I understand. Ashley patted his hand. "Two hours early? Okay. I'll be ready. You won't forget me, will you?"

Harry lurched forward and took her hands. They were shaking. "Never, ever." He touched her cheek, then turned and ran out.

Ashley noted the care in Ellie's eyes. "He's really a great guy, just a little shy. Don't give up on him."

Ashley's cheek still tingled from the warmth of his touch. "Never." *Ever.*

Chapter 4

*H*arry's heart was in his throat as he stood outside the door looking into the tea shop. *What in the world?* All three women had on the strangest hats, like woolen caps, but with bright, merry fabric. They were laughing. Harry opened the door.

Ashley turned to him, her face smiling with joy. "Harry. Like my new hat?"

She's so beautiful. "Quite fetching. Never saw one like that."

Sophie was laughing. "They're the new teapot covers. The ones Ashley picked out for my shop. Decided to give them a go. Want to join the party?"

Before Harry had a chance to answer, Ashley grabbed another cover from a box. She had to stand on her tiptoes to reach his head and gently placed it there. Her eyes were sparkling. "You look like a king. Look everyone, my King Harry has arrived."

Both Ellie and Sophie grew quiet. Harry noticed both sets of eyes were open wide.

Ashley gently touched his arm. "Do with me what you want, my king."

It took everything he had not to kiss those cute little lips. Instead, he engulfed Ashley with a deep hug. "In my eyes, you're the one who is royalty, my princess." His lips gently grazed her ear. "You are absolutely perfect in every way."

She pulled back and stared at him, wonder in her eyes. "Harry, I, uh..."

He kissed her hand and bowed. "My lady, your chariot awaits." She reached for the cover on her head. "Keep it there. I like being your king... and you, my princess."

Her face lit up like a Christmas tree. Harry truly felt like royalty when she put her arm through his.

As they were walking out the door, Sophie yelled after them. "Don't worry about us. We'll be just fine."

Harry ignored her.

Ashley bit her lip when he held the truck door. He circled around then climbed in next to her.

The anticipation was quite evident in her face. "Finally, we're alone. Are you going to ask me now? I've been waiting all day to find out what it is."

He turned to her. Ashley's eyes glittered like gems. Harry reached for her hands. So soft and warm. "I, uh, this might not come out right. Ashley, I want to share some things with you, so you can understand me better." He grimaced. *Harder than I thought.* Her eyes changed, so full of enchantment.

She stared at him. "Your, your words, they're different. Not so gruff. Why did you change? Sophie told me you didn't talk like everyone else because, uh, you know."

Harry laughed. "I don't doubt she did say that. I mince words because I'm afraid what I have to say isn't important to anyone."

Ashley's eyes showed her honesty as she squeezed his hands tightly. "But it is. J-just like you are... to me."

He had to take a deep breath. "I know. Important, to you. Exactly as you are to me." Her face was so beautiful. "Ashley, I want you to know me, not the same old me everyone sees, but the real me. And I wanted to ask if I can introduce you to my family. I want them to meet you, to see how wonderful and beautiful and kind and special and lovable you are."

She turned away. "Thank you, but you don't have to say that. I'm just a frail, sickly girl. I can't see how anyone could ever love me." Ashley's face reddened when she realized what she'd said.

Harry's voice was barely above a whisper. "I can't see how everyone couldn't help but love you."

Her mouth dropped open. She studied his eyes.

"I want you to know more about me before, before I..."

Her eyes were glued to his face. "Before..."

He had to close his eyes to gather his strength. "I want to c-court you, Ashley."

Her head jerked. "Court me? What's that?"

"I think the American phrase is to 'date you'. The saddest part of my week is when I drop you off on Friday night. I miss you on the weekends. I, oh, let me be frank. I want to see more of you... and before I do, I want you to know the real me. So you can tell if you really want to be with me."

Ashley gently touched his face. "You should know by now, I do. I know all I need to know about you. You're kind and gentle and oh so handsome. Not to mention special and wonderful."

Harry looked away. "I'm not handsome."

"Okay, gorgeous then."

He felt his cheeks heat.

A smile graced those beautiful lips. "And I know something else about you. I know your deepest, darkest secret."

Harry's eyes involuntarily widened. "You know my secret?" *How could you?*

She giggled and moved her head so their noses touched. "Yep. You're a pot head."

"What?"

"Uh-huh. Proof's on your head."

Ashley started laughing and Harry joined her. Her hands touched his head as she drew his face to hers. Her laughter was gone. "The real secret is you're a true king. My king." Ashley gulped and quickly kissed his lips. "The king of my heart."

***

Ashley knew any second now she'd wake and find this was a dream. Just like the fantasies that filled her nights. But the manly taste of his lips lingered on her tongue. *Kiss me again so I know this is real.* As if in response, Harry lowered his mouth to hers. As they kissed, she breathed in his scent. *So manly, yet fragrant.*

Harry murmured, "I've dreamed about our first kiss for so long. The actual is so much better than my hopes." Harry kissed her again, even more softly. He

36

pulled away. "Please tell me this hat you gave me isn't giving me delusions. Tell me this is really happening."

Ashley's lips found his. "Feels real to me." The corner of her eye detected movement. The sight before her made her mouth dry. Still parked in front of the tea room, Sophie and Ellie were watching. Not just watching, but gesturing. Sophie was pumping her fists and Ellie was dancing around as she waved her arms over her head.

Harry's face blushed. "Damned paparazzi. So hard for royals like us to have a special moment."

Ashley slid across the bench seat so she could snuggle with him as he drove. *Like I was meant to be here.* She still clung to him when he parked in front of one of the glass houses on the farm.

As he opened her door, he removed his hat and bowed. "Princess?"

Her heart was beating so loud she was having trouble hearing. "Why are we here?"

Harry took her arm. "I have four passions in my life. You just found out the first one."

She stopped and searched his face. "I did?"

Harry kissed her hand. "Yes. My first and most important passion is you." Ashley's heart raced. His lips squeezed together. The way his eyes touched her face made her feel faint. "It will take me a while to show you my fourth passion, but my second is my family. I can't wait to show you off."

Ashley's chest was on fire. *His family?* He led her into the building. It was warm, yet a heavenly fragrance filled the air, his scent. "First, second, fourth. What's your third passion?"

Harry smiled as he opened the door. "These."

She stepped into a room filled with a kaleidoscope of colorful flowers. "What are these?"

"Passion number three. My gladiolas. Aren't they beautiful?"

"Beautiful isn't the right word. They're spectacular."

Harry removed a knife from his pocket and cut down an armful. He turned to her. "Yes, they are spectacular and beautiful, but they can't compare to you. These are for my princess."

He handed them to her. Everything became blurry. "Harry..."

He pushed her hair behind her ears and then lifted her chin so they were looking eye to eye. "You're crying. Did I do something to upset you?"

She shook her head. "Not at all."

"Then what's wrong? Is it me?"

Ashley surprised herself when she set the flowers down and threw her arms around him. "Yes. Yes, it's you."

He pulled away and his face was pale.

"Some-something wrong with me? Don't you like me?"

"No."

Harry's mouth dropped open. "No?"

She couldn't help but smile. "No, there's nothing wrong with you. Yes, I like you, a whole lot. It's just, well..."

His big thumbs were so gentle when he brushed her tears aside. "Just what?"

She choked back a sob. "These flowers... first time anyone gave me flowers." She again wrapped her arms around this man she realized she loved. "Thank you, Harry. You really are a king and I'm a princess, aren't I?"

Harry softly kissed her. "Yes, you are the princess of my heart."

***

Sophie sat alone on the porch, her eyes searching the stars. Her hands were warmed by the hot tea in her cup. The screen door closed softly behind her.

Ben sat down and pulled her toward him. Sophie fought back the tears.

"Maybe it's time we moved."

"Moved? But this is your home."

"No, it's our home. But seeing Ellie grow bigger every day is wearing on you."

"No, that's not it at all."

Ben sniffed. "Guess you're right. It's not Ellie. It's me." He shifted position and held her hands. "Sophia, you're my every dream come true. My greatest blessing in life has been sharing it with you. But, but maybe it's time to let you go. So you can find someone who can really make you happy. Someone who can give you children. Someone who can..."

Her bitterness and anger boiled out of control. "You bloody idiot. How can you... How could you think I'd ever want any man but you?"

"I can't give you..."

She pushed him away. The hot tears running down her cheeks seared her skin. "If that's all you think I care about, damn you. I love you, you idiot. No. It's time for me to give up on my dream. I don't want to be a mother anymore. Not if it means losing you. How could you even think that?"

Sophie threw her teacup in the yard and ran to the bathroom, locking the door behind her.

Almost immediately, Ben started knocking on the door. "Sophie, let me in. We need to talk."

Her voice was unsteady. "Not tonight. The time for talking is past."

Sophie cried herself to sleep on the bathroom floor, but the last thing she heard were Ben's sobs, just a few feet away.

Chapter 5

*H*arry ran his finger in between the collar and his neck. *Hate stupid ties.* He parked the truck in front of Ashley's house. Ellie had loaned him her customized SUV because his old pickup wasn't good enough, not to take Ashley and her mother out.

He said a quick prayer before he knocked on the door. *Talk natural, out of respect. Long sentences.* His jaw dropped when Ashley opened it. *Heaven must be missing an angel.* She was wearing a simple pink dress, but wore it like a goddess. Ashley quickly kissed his cheek.

The sound of someone clearing her throat caught his attention. A middle-aged woman stood slightly behind Ashley. Her face sported a frown.

"Harry, I'd like you to meet my mother, Jessica Snyder. Mom, this is Harry Campbell."

Harry bowed. "Mrs. Snyder, it's an honor to meet you."

She still didn't smile as she assessed him. Her gaze made him feel naked. She extended her hand. "Mr. Campbell. Last night was the first time I'd heard about you or what my daughter has been doing behind my back for the last several weeks. Just so you know, I don't like surprises. Especially not when it comes to Ashley. I am not happy, sir."

He forced a smile. "I understand, ma'am. That's why I asked both of you to dinner."

The puzzlement in Mrs. Snyder's face was evident. "Explain yourself."

His cheeks were heating. "We both feel the same about our families, protective. If the roles were reversed, I'd also be skeptical. I'm hoping that tonight, you'll get to know me and give your blessing to my proposition."

Her face reddened. "What proposition?"

"Mrs. Snyder. I really like your daughter and I'm, uh, I really want to ask if you'll, uh, let me..."

Her stare could make milk curdle. "No. You can't marry her. I won't allow it."

Harry gulped hard. "I, uh, did you say marriage?"

"That's right. Let me save you the cost of taking me out to dinner. No, no, no and no. I don't even know you and yet you want to..."

He held up his hands. "I think you misunderstood me."

Jessica Snyder crossed her arms. "Go on."

"I want to court, I mean, date your daughter. Not marry her." *Yet*.

Her face turned pink. "I'm sorry. Guess I jumped to conclusions."

Harry hoped his smile appeared as genuine as he meant it. "That's all right, ma'am. Your daughter deserves respect. And from me, she'll always get it. I'll guarantee it."

Mrs. Snyder shook her head. "You don't know her. She gets sick, quite frequently. She had cancer..."

His voice was soft. "I know."

Ashley put her hand to her mouth. "You knew?"

Harry touched her face. "Ellie told me."

Ashley started to back away from him. "This, this was all because you pitied me? I thought you really..."

He quickly strode forward and took her hand. "Stop. Right now. I do care and not because you were sick. I was attracted to you long before I knew about the cancer."

Ashley's eyes widened. "You were? When?"

He glanced at his watch. "Fifty-one days, seven hours and uh, thirty-six minutes ago."

"What?"

"That's the moment I first saw you along the road."

***

Jessica Snyder sat on the chair waiting for her daughter to come in after saying goodnight. *Misjudged that boy.* He might have looked big and tough, but he wore his heart on his sleeve.

While she waited, she chanced a glance in the mirror. *I'm still kind of pretty.* Young enough to have a life. It wasn't that she didn't love Ashley, she was just weary of taking care of her. Ever since her daughter had been diagnosed with cancer at age six, every minute of Jessica's life had been spent taking care of Ashley. When her husband Cameron died unexpectedly of a heart attack two years ago, she'd also had to become the bread winner. Maybe now she'd finally get a chance to enjoy and live her own life.

The sound of tires on stones caught her attention. Jessica's eye tracked to her daughter. Ashley was inside, waving at the man who had swept both of them off their feet tonight. Ashley closed the door and leaned with her back against it. Jessica could see the stars in her daughter's eyes.

Ashley's voice came out softly. "Oh, Mom. Did tonight really happen?"

Jessica touched her daughter's nose. "Come down off cloud nine. Welcome back to earth."

Ashley grabbed her arms. "Tell me you liked him."

"He did seem nice."

"Nice? Come on. He answered everything you threw at him."

"That he did."

"And you said he could date me, didn't you?"

Jessica bit her lip to keep from laughing.

"Thank you, Mom."

"Just be careful you don't get hurt."

"He'd never hurt me. He loves me." Ashley's hands flew to her mouth.

Jessica could see it. Her heart fluttered for her daughter. She extended her hands. Ashley quickly took them. "Did he tell you that?"

"He didn't have to."

"No, he didn't. People flying from New York to Los Angeles could see how much he loves you. He even remembered the date and time he met you."

Ashley wiped her arm across her eyes. "I love him, too."

Jessica smiled. "Even people in China could see that."

***

Edmund stood in the darkening night. The contrasting scents of fresh cut alfalfa and burning wood filled the air. Flames lit the outdoor fireplace in the backyard where the family was gathered. Not where he wanted to be, but Tara was doing her once a month Saturday night rotation at the hospital.

He sauntered over, plopping in one of the wicker chairs. "Hey, Mum."

Darcy turned and grasped his hand. "My baby boy. How be you?"

"Tired. Mum, I'm twenty-four. Quit calling me your baby."

She pinched his cheek. "You'll always be my baby."

He kissed her hand. "Thought Maggot was your wee one."

Margaret laughed. "I used to be, but it seems I've been replaced."

Darcy half-heartedly admonished her, "Now don't be jealous, lass. I've not even met the girl yet."

Ellie's giggle filled Edmund's ears. "You'll love her, guaranteed. Childlike innocence, but with a maturity beyond her years."

Who are they talking about?

Margaret's voice was quieter. "I'm so happy for Harry. Seems so in love."

Edmund cleared his throat. "Harry? In love? Did I miss something?"

Darcy patted his hand. "Your brother's met a young lass. She's been spending her days keeping company at the Tea Room. According to your sister-in-law, the situation's quite serious. Henry and Margaret have a little bet as to how soon he'll ask for her hand."

Edmund's mouth was dry. Harry's that serious about a girl? And no one had thought to tell him? *What am I, chopped liver?* If Harry got engaged first, Tara would be intolerable. "Didn't know he had a steady. How long's this been going on? What else have I missed?"

Henry stood, handed Edmund a cold bottle of ale and threw more wood on the fire. "Depends. Are you talking about the family or the business?"

"Family."

"I think you'll be getting a new sister-in-law before the end of the year. Of course, Maggot thinks it will be within the next two months."

Edmund choked on his drink. "Next two months? Did he get her in trouble?"

Henry's voice was icy. "No. Harry reveres her, like men are *supposed* to treat women."

You and your sense of honor. Edmund's cheeks heated. "Something you're trying to say to me?"

Henry turned and walked until they were face to face. "I believe you're bright enough to read between the lines. Too bad you've no respect for Tara."

Edmund's fists curled into balls. He wanted to punch his brother, but knew he was no match for Henry, the ex-Royal Marine. "Not everyone can be as perfect as you or Harry. It's been miserable, growing up in the shadows of such legends."

"Shadows of legends? Don't follow our footsteps. Blaze your own trail, just don't disgrace the family. Excellence runs in your blood. I'm sure even you feel it." In the flickering firelight, Henry's hands were also curling into fists.

Ellie extracted herself from her chair and waddled over to stand between them. "Henry, Edmund, behave like the loving brothers you are."

Edmund really liked Ellie, but her apricot-scented essence fueled his anger. "Pity your pregnant wife has to come to your rescue."

Henry tried to sidestep Ellie to reach him. No doubt Henry wanted to give him a thrashing – that was plain to see. Normally, Edmund would be running for his life, but Ellie would prevent it. His brother's wife wrapped her arms around Henry. Edmund smiled with disdain as Henry's expression calmed in her embrace.

Wimp. He decided to take a step closer to get under his brother's skin, but long, strong arms grasped his midsection. Margaret.

"Calm down. He didn't mean it the way it sounded, did you?"

Even in the dim light, Edmund could see Henry's lips were set in a fine line. Firm fingers grasped his ear as Darcy grabbed both of her sons. "I'll have none of this. Henry, apologize to him, now."

Henry took a deep breath. "I'm sorry, Edmund."

Edmund didn't bother to reply as he peeled Margaret's arms away. Darcy pinched his ear even tighter. "And what do you have to say to Henry?"

Screw you, brother. "Apology accepted."

"And..."

"Sorry."

"Now both of you shake hands."

Henry extended his hand first. Edmund had to breathe deeply before taking it.

Henry's voice was calmer. "I'm truly sorry for how it sounded. Please forgive me."

Edmund cocked his head. "Forgive me, too. Sorry I'm not exactly how you want me to be. 'Night, everyone."

***

Harry touched Ashley's hand. "You look beautiful today." And she did. Jessica had done her hair, pinning it into a bun. The white dress with cherry clusters on it was lucky to be wrapped around her slight frame. Harry had never seen anyone look as wonderful as she did.

Ashley was biting her lips. "Do you think your mom and sister will like me?"

"They will love you... like..."

Ashley touched his face. "Yes?"

Harry wanted to tell her so badly, but not just yet. He needed to know for sure Ashley felt the same. "They'll love you like crazy."

She smiled. "Liar. You can't fool me. That's not what you were going to say, was it?"

He kissed her pretty lips. "No, it wasn't. I can't and don't want to, ever... fool you, that is."

"Never, ever?"

Harry wrapped his arms around her and held her tightly. "Never, ever, forever. Do you know how I feel about you?"

Her eyes sparkled. "I think so."

Harry was having trouble keeping it inside. He lowered his lips to Ashley's. "You are perfect, in every way. Do you know that?"

She kissed him back and giggled. "You're good at changing the subject. Tell me. What were you going to say?"

No secrets, not from you. He framed her face with his hands. *Here goes.* "I'm in love with you, Ashley."

Ashley's face blanched and her eyes widened. Fear tingled up Harry's spine. *I was wrong.* Suddenly, a wide smile covered her face and she kissed him deeply. The wonder in her eyes took his breath away. "I'm in love with you, too!"

***

Ellie was having a wonderful time. Her two favorite aunts, Kaitlin and Kelly had come to visit. Their husbands were in the next room chatting with Henry.

Kaitlin plopped in the easy chair. "Wow. This place is amazing. How many bedrooms does this house have?"

"Ten. Each with a private bath."

Kelly took a sip of her diet cola. "That leaves nine rooms for kids. Of course you know, twins run in the family. Eighteen kids. Thought Geeter and I had our hands full with six."

Before Ellie could answer, Henry's mother Darcy and his sister Margaret brought in a tray of snacks. Ellie grabbed a small Danish off the tray before Margaret could set it down.

Darcy gently smacked her hand. "Where are your manners, girl? Didn't I teach you better than that? Guests should..." Darcy stopped in mid-sentence. Her mouth dropped open.

Ellie turned to see what she was staring at. In the door frame stood Harry and Ashley. Ellie's jaw also fell open. Ashley looked like she'd just stepped off the runway. Her hair was perfect, makeup exquisite and she wore a dress most women would die for. *Is this the same little girl who hangs with us?* On her shoulder was a corsage made of gladiolas. *Harry's flowers?* But something else was there, something special. *Love?* Ellie shifted her gaze to Harry, dressed in a charming gray suit. He'd never looked so happy or confident. *Definitely love.*

Darcy walked to the pair. Her voice exuded amazement. "Glory be, child! Aren't you a sight for sore eyes? Harry, you told me you'd met a lass, but you held back." Darcy crushed Ashley in her arms. "I'm Darcy, Harry's mum. You should call me Mum, too."

The sweet scent of the gladiolas tickled Ellie's nose. *Ashley's perfume or the fragrance of the flowers?* Less than four years ago, that had been her in Darcy's embrace. Ellie wondered what Ashley thought of it all.

Fingers touched Ellie's shoulder. Margaret.

"Looks like we're getting another sister. Hope she's as nice as you."

Ellie squeezed her hand in return. "Thanks, sis. The way she looks, I'm envious. Even Sophie never looked that classy. And Harry? Look at that smile." Ellie turned when she heard Margaret sniff.

Margaret wiped her sleeve over her eyes. "I'm so happy for him. Told me he's finally over her."

"You mean Tara?"

"Yes. He also told me he's in love with Ashley. Excuse me, I've got to meet her." Margaret walked over to stand in line behind Ellie's aunts, who had also sauntered over to greet Harry and Ashley.

Ashley stopped her conversation with Kaitlin when she noticed Margaret. She stepped forward and took Harry's sister's hands. "You, you've got to be Margaret. Even prettier than Harry said." Ashley wrapped her arms around her. "I'm so glad to finally meet you. Harry's been bragging you up, but he didn't do you justice."

Ellie snickered at the blush on Margaret's face.

Margaret had such a big smile. "Ashley, he didn't say how enchanting you were, either. It's so good to finally meet you. We're going to be such good friends."

The two women talked as if no one else was around. "I hope we'll become best friends. And maybe you can fill me in on your brother. Ellie and Sophie gave me opposing views. Ellie says he can almost walk on water, yet Sophie acts like he's some backwoods hick. Maybe you'll tell me the truth."

Harry's face was pink. He interrupted them. "Now ladies, Mum has gone to all this trouble to make us some treats. Let's take a few minutes to enjoy these delicacies."

Margaret shot Ellie a wink. "The first thing, Ashley, is that he always tries to move the conversation away from himself. Let's talk privately." Margaret linked her arm through Ashley's and led her away. Fright covered the big man's face.

Ellie walked over and touched Harry's hand. "Don't worry. I'll keep the stories in line." She paused to study his expression. "You look so happy."

"I am and th-thanks. Don't let Maggot get too carried away. I'll have to live up to whatever she tells Ashley."

The women planned on spending the afternoon having tea at Sophie's shop. The men were heading off to see the operation. Ellie picked up on Harry's look of longing when they parted.

Kaitlin must have noted it, too. She turned to Ellie. "*Hmm.* Harry reminds me of your husband, and Ashley? The look on her face reminds me of yours whenever you look at Henry. Let's keep up with them. I want to get all the juicy gossip on this budding romance."

Henry came over to kiss Ellie goodbye. She could feel his devilry. "So my brother almost walks on water, huh?"

She kissed him fully on the lips. "Yes, he's almost perfect. But remember, in my eyes, the only perfect man is you."

Chapter 6

llie's chest warmed as Henry kissed her lips. "Aren't you the vision of loveliness today?"

"How can you always be so kind to me?"

He held her. "That's easy. You're perfect and besides that, we're one."

Ellie knew her twin dimples were making an appearance.

Henry cleared his throat. "Something's bothering you. What is it?"

She laughed at him. That ability to read each other's feelings was such a blessing. "I still can't understand how you do that."

"Do what?"

"Read my mind."

"It's a blessing from God. Now what's going on in your beautiful head?"

Ellie touched his cheek. "You tell me."

Henry studied her eyes momentarily. "Edmund. And the fact that he's up to his old tricks again. Being a jerk, especially to Harry."

"You *can* read my mind. I'm concerned about Edmund's change in behavior. It started that night at the campfire. What's going on?"

Henry stood and offered his hand. He'd felt she was going to stand. "Don't know for sure, but I assume he and Tara are having a spat. About what, I don't know. I can't read him like I can you."

Thank God. "Maybe Tara's upset he hasn't proposed. They've been dating for three years."

Henry's face clouded. "I believe the little demon is doing more than dating her."

Now she read his thoughts. "Henry! Just because they aren't like us..."

His voice sported anger. "If he honored her like we did each other, he'd have waited."

"They're not us." The warmth of his feelings touched her.

"Suppose not, but I thought I brought him up better than that."

The care Henry had for both his brothers came through to her. "I forgot you were like a father to him when your pops died."

"Tried to be a role model. Harry seemed to come out okay."

"Except for the part where he gives it back to Edmund every chance he gets. I was really hoping Edmund would bring Tara over to meet my aunts last month. You know..."

Henry smiled. "Yes, Tara's like a sister to you. Your chosen sister. Should I talk to him?"

Ellie weighed the thought of it in her mind. "Not yet. I just hope he comes around. Perhaps..." The baby suddenly started to jump in her belly. Ellie didn't have to say a thing.

Henry fell to his knees, lips against her stomach. "Maggie, be gentle. You're making Mummy uncomfortable."

Ellie laughed. "Don't listen to your old dad. I'm your mommy, not mummy."

Henry kissed her belly and the movement inside was indeed gentler. "That's my girl. Always listen to your mommy."

Ellie giggled. "You certainly do have a way with women."

His smile was dazzling. "Maybe just with one, but only time will tell."

***

Harry loved the feel of Ashley's body leaning against him as they drove home after visiting Margaret at State College. "Do you know how much I love you, Ashley?"

"Love you too, Harry. Hey, I'm not feeling so good. Think we could stop and get something to drink?"

"Sure, princess. Where don't you feel well?"

"I've got a headache, my throat's sore and I'm freezing."

Harry felt her forehead. "You're burning up. How long ago did this start?"

"I dunno. Couple minutes." Ashley pulled away and watched his face. "Do you know your love is the best thing to ever happen to me? Promise me you'll always remember how much I love you. And that you'll never forget me. Never. Ever."

Her words made his eyes scratchy. "Please, don't talk like that. I'll be with you, forever. That's a promise. I could never forget you."

Ashley's voice was soft. "Never, ever?"

"Never. Ever. Forever and ever. I love you, Ashley. What can I do to help you?"

"Call my mom. I think I'm getting sick again."

***

Harry stood as the nurse approached. His heart was in his throat. Mrs. Snyder had met them at the hospital and went back with Ashley into the Emergency Department, over an hour ago. "Mr. Campbell? Please follow me." She led him back a hallway and held open a curtain. "They're in here."

Jessica Snyder was sitting next to Ashley. Ashley's slight frame barely filled a quarter of the bed. She forced a smile when Harry entered. "Not how you wanted to spend tonight, huh?"

Harry kissed her forehead. "It's okay. How are you?"

Mrs. Snyder answered for her. "It's only a virus, thank God. But there's something I have to tell you. With all the treatments Ashley's gone through in her life, her immune system is weak. It takes a while to fight off infections. When she gets sick like this, it might take her three weeks to recover from what a normal person could handle in two or three days."

Harry listened, but his eyes were on Ashley. She looked so sad. "Sorry, Harry."

He squeezed her hand. "Don't be, princess."

Mrs. Snyder's voice quivered as she continued to speak. "She'll need constant care and since I work, I can't do it. I'll see if Mrs. Eschelman can watch her again. I'll get fired if I skip work that long."

Harry's heart went out to Ashley when he saw the look of despair on his girl's face. "Please Mom, don't send me there. Her boys torment me and I can't rest."

Mrs. Snyder's face aged in front of him. "Honey, it's the best I can do."

Ashley wiped her cheek. "I know, but maybe I could stay home, by myself."

"Ash, you can't. You need someone there. I would if I could, but..."

Ashley needs me. Harry spoke up. "Let me stay with her."

Both women looked at him in astonishment. Jessica shook her head. "That's generous, but you're working and..."

"I can stay with her when you aren't there. I'll work at night. Henry will let me."

"And if he won't let you?"

"I'll ask Ellie. She always says family is the most important thing in the world. She'll support me."

Mrs. Snyder frowned. "You don't know how to care for her."

"I'm a quick study and if I need help, there's my mum and Ellie and..."

"No. I appreciate the offer, but..."

Harry touched the mother's arm. "I promise I'll take good care of her. I love your daughter. I'll do anything for her."

Mrs. Snyder shook her head. "Harry, I..."

"Look. Let me take care of her for two days. If I don't... If you think I'm not taking good enough care of Ashley, then take her where you planned. I have to tell you though, I will be there with her every day. She may be your little girl, but she's my entire world."

Mrs. Snyder's eyes bore into Harry's soul, searching, assessing everything.

Ashley's voice broke the trance. "Mom? I'm nineteen. Please let me have a say in this. I don't want to stay with the Eschelmans. I'd like Harry to take care of me."

The mother's bottom lip stuck out as she gazed at Ashley's face. Harry could see her eyes tear. *Poor woman. So tough doing this alone.* A sob escaped her mouth. "I've tried my best to be a good mother..."

His heart went out to her. Harry instinctively wrapped his arms around Mrs. Snyder. "And you are. Let me help. I promise I'll always be here. Together, the three of us can do anything."

***

The world slowly rolled into focus. Ashley could hear Harry breathing rhythmically. He was catching up on his sleep. *Thank you, God.* For the last two and a half weeks, Harry had been by her side from seven every morning until he left for work at nine at night. She was in the same position she'd assumed during that time period. Her head was on his right leg, left arm folded back over her right shoulder, fingers entwined with his.

He shifted slightly. Ashley turned to study his face. So regal. He'd cared for her unceasingly. She'd never felt as loved as she did right now. Ashley softly touched his face.

Harry stirred at her touch, immediately waking. "Princess. What can I get you?"

"How about a kiss?"

His smile set her heart on fire, not to mention the feel of his lips on hers. "Princess, you're perfect." Harry's eyes shined brightly in the afternoon light, but then his face showed something she hadn't seen before. "I need you, Ashley. I feel so alive when I'm with you. The last two weeks made me realize something. I want a life with you."

Her heart skipped a beat. "A, a life? With me? What's that mean?"

"I want to marry you."

Ashley's eyes involuntarily widened. "Marriage? I, uh, Harry, I don't..."

He touched her lips. "I don't mean to spring this on you, but I want you to know my intentions. Marriage is the most sacred thing in the world to me. Sharing everything in life with one person and only one person. Making a life just the two of us would share is my greatest dream. I want my life to be spent only with you."

The world was spinning. *Not even in my wildest dreams...* "But suppose I get sick again? I mean really sick, like cancer."

"Then I'll be here. With you, forever. That's my promise, to you. Forever and ever. For always. Until the day I quit breathing."

"Are you proposing to me?"

Harry's smile was enchanting. "Not yet. I just wanted you to know it's coming. I hope you feel the same way as I do. And when I do propose, I promise it will be special. Something deserving of my princess."

Ashley's vision blurred as fear entered her heart. *But you don't know the truth yet.* "But suppose…"

"I don't care. I love you. I'll be here." His hands framed her face. "Always."

Ashley wrapped her arms around him. "Can I tell you a secret?"

"Please do."

"When you ask, the answer will be yes."

Effortlessly, Harry lifted her body so she was sitting on his lap. "Princess, you're the answer to my every prayer. I'm so glad I found you." His lips sought hers.

"I love you. I couldn't be happier. Never dreamed I'd find someone who would…" Ashley choked up.

His smile melted away her fears. "Just hold on. You have my word. Each day will be better than the day before. Ever and forever."

Chapter 7

The wonderful aromas coming from the kitchen tickled Ellie's senses. Darcy was cooking for the company picnic. Ellie rolled over in bed, trying to find a comfortable position. She'd gained almost thirty pounds during her pregnancy. *Hope it comes off as quickly as it went on.*

A voice floated from the other side of the bed. "Good morning, honey. I brought you coffee. Would you like a sip?" Ellie smiled as she gazed into the intense green Scottish eyes of her love, her Henry. She nodded. He reached in to give her a mind blowing kiss. "You look so beautiful. Have I told you that lately?"

Ellie laughed. Henry, her every dream come true. Never had she imagined finding someone who could make her feel like he did. Her mind drifted back to the night they'd first met. Henry had looked so attractive and when he kissed her hand that night, she'd already felt love in her heart for him. Then, on their first date at Diana's memorial, he'd dried her feet after their picnic. She'd seen love in his eyes that evening. That was the day she realized he was in love with her, too.

She reached for Henry's hand. Their love had grown quickly and deeply. Henry and his sister Margaret had been the ones who rescued her when she'd been kidnapped. Henry had offered his own life as a sacrifice for her freedom. She'd almost lost him that night, but God brought him through. Ellie knew her twin dimples were showing. Henry always found a way to make every day more magical than the one before. Such a romantic. And the way they could read each other's feelings...

He kissed her fingers. "I love you, too."

Ellie laughed. "You always tell me you love me first thing in the morning and at least twenty times a day. I hope you know I love you more than any man has ever been loved before in the history of the universe."

Henry kissed her again, his lips gently pulling at hers as he moved away. "You probably tell that to every man you wake up next to in the morning." He handed her the cup of coffee, prepared exactly as she liked it.

She winked at him. "That's right. I tell that to every single one of them. All one of them." Pain radiated across her mid-section. "Henry..." Her little girl was really active this morning. "Our little Maggie will be a gymnast. She's doing floor exercises this morning."

Henry stood. "What can I do?"

She grasped his hand tightly as the baby did cartwheels inside of her. "Just you being with me, that's all I need. I wouldn't go through this with anyone but you. Mind helping me to the bathroom?"

"Absolutely. I can help you shower, too, if you'd like." He pulled back her covers and effortlessly picked her up in his arms and headed toward their private bath.

She whispered in his ear, "I'd love that. You're so wonderful. You turn me on so much. If I wasn't so fat, ugly and uncomfortable, I'd..." Ellie whispered her thoughts into his ear.

Henry rubbed his nose against hers. "You aren't fat, and you certainly aren't ugly. You are beauty beyond measure. I'll take a raincheck. I hope you realize that isn't why I love you, don't you?"

Ellie's hands cupped his face. "Yes. What we have is so special."

Henry helped Ellie to shower. As he dried her back, she studied her body in the mirror. *My belly looks different.* She wondered when the baby would come. Ellie hoped Maggie would wait until after the picnic to make her entrance.

***

Benjamin Miller leaned up against the kitchen counter, watching as Sophie made their breakfast. Frustration was boiling over inside him. He loved Sophie, but *his* issue was causing problems between them. He set down his cup, walked over to the stove and held her in his arms. The tears Sophie had fought to hold back all morning came out in full force.

"Sophie, I'm sorry."

Her sadness wet his shoulder. "It's not your fault. I've told you that time and again. I don't blame this on you. At all."

"I know, but my inability to father a child is driving a wedge between us. Let's talk about adoption again."

She shook her head violently. "No! I don't want to adopt a child. I want to carry a child, our child, and give birth. Can we talk about artificial insemination again?"

"Yes, we can. I'm all for it."

"As long as it's someone you don't know, you're fine with it. Please see my side of things."

Anger built in him, not at Sophie, but at the situation. He had to be careful here. It seemed every time they discussed it, he lost his temper and took it out on her. Couldn't she see how much of a compromise it would be for her to carry a child that wasn't his? To top it off, she'd already chosen whom she wanted to be the donor. "Soph, I don't want to fight about this again."

She looked him squarely in his eyes, "It's bad enough the child won't have your genes. I want the father to be someone I know. Suppose the child has a problem where the donor..."

Ben's sight grew blurry. "It won't be our child, Sophie, it will be your child and..."

"Poppycock, Benjy. The child will be ours. Ours, do you get it? There is so much more to being a father than supplying the seed and you know it."

"Right. You should have married him. I bet if you knew I was sterile, you wouldn't have married me."

Sophie shoved his body away from her. "Listen, Benjy. I chose you and would every time. It's you I want to spend my life with. You I want to raise our children with."

Ben wiped his cheeks and turned from her.

"Look at me, Benjy!" She grasped his head so he was staring solely into her eyes. "Even if I would have known, I still would have married you. I love you and only you. Get that through your skull. If I had my choice of every man in this world, it would always be you."

He couldn't help the moisture in his eyes. "If that's true, then explain why you are so adamant to have Henry Campbell father your child."

***

A few hours later, Sophie walked outside to help Harry with the final preparations for the company picnic. Sadness filled her soul. While Darcy was preparing the food, Harry and Sophie were in charge of getting everything ready. Edmund was supposed to be helping, but as usual, he was nowhere to be found.

Sophie had no merriment in her voice. "Where is your worthless brother this morning?"

Harry shrugged his shoulders, but didn't respond.

"Harry, did you unlock the barn and turn on the air?"

"Yes."

"I didn't see Ellie yet today, did you?"

"No."

"Can you say more than one word at a time?"

"Yes."

"Then why the hell don't you?" She burst into tears.

Harry stopped what he was doing. He approached and reached for her. She quickly clung to him. "I offended you. Didn't mean to. What's wrong?"

She suddenly pushed him away. "You'd never understand. I need someone to talk to me and it's no use asking you. I don't think you've said more than ten words to me in your entire life."

Harry stared at her. "Never said much because I didn't think you liked me. I'm sorry. Should I get Ellie?"

She sobbed harshly. "I can't talk to her about this. I can't talk to anyone."

Harry extended his hands to Sophie. "I'm here. What's wrong?"

"Like you'd understand." She slapped his hands away. "You're just plain mean, and, and simple. A man of no feelings." Her tears were flowing hard.

Harry softly grasped her hands. "I am a man of few words, but don't think just because I don't say much, I don't feel inside. I give you a hard time because I like you. If that came across as being mean, forgive me. If you need a friend, you have one. I'll help any way I can. What's bothering you?"

Sophie looked at him for a moment, trying to decide if she wanted to tell him. She needed to get this off her chest. "What I have to say, no one can ever know. I don't know if I can trust you."

His hard face softened. "Lots of secrets around here, but I'll never tell anyone, not Ellie, Henry,

Maggot or even Ashley. The decision's yours, but if you need a friend, I'm here."

The door suddenly flew open and in strolled Edmund. Harry quickly let go of Sophie's hand, but not before Edmund noted it. "Well, well, what did I stumble upon?"

Sophie's face turned bright red. In anger, she turned her wrath on Edmund. "Where the bloody hell have you been all morning? You're supposed to be out here helping us."

Edmund leered at her. "I was getting a little loving from your sister-in-law. You know, something to start the weekend." Sophie glanced at Harry, seeing anger lurking in his eyes. Edmund laughed. "Actually, it was more than a little. Shall I tell you what we did?" Edmund watched Harry's face with glee. Harry's jaw clenched, as did his fists.

Both Harry and Sophie yelled in unison, "No!"

Edmund polished his fingernails on his shirt. "Heard you had a girlfriend, Harry. Didn't know it was Ben's wife. How long have you two been doing it?"

Sophie's anger exploded. "You're a little snipe, Edmund. If you weren't Henry's brother, I would scratch your eyes out."

Edmund laughed. "Oh, poo poo. Should I give the two of you five minutes to finish, or do you need less time than that, Harry?"

Sophie hissed at him. "Get your dirty mind out of the gutter. We were just talking. And since you came so late, you can finish setting up by yourself." She handed him a piece of paper. "Here's the list of what has to be done. Get moving or I *will* tell Ellie and Henry on you."

Edmund looked at the long list in dismay. "Wait. Maybe the three of us can split up the work."

Harry took a menacing step toward his younger brother. Edmund's face showed fear. "No. Earn your keep. Do it yourself. Or else."

Edmund apparently knew enough to back down. Harry obviously meant business. Edmund took the list and headed out of the barn, slamming the door behind him.

After he left, Sophie eyed Harry. "Secrets? I think you might have one of your own, don't you?"

Harry's eyes questioned her. "What do you mean?"

"I saw how you reacted when Edmund was talking about Tara. You care for her, don't you?"

Harry closed his eyes, breathing deeply. "At one time I did, before Ashley. Hurts to hear him talk about Tara that way. Please don't say anything."

Sophie laughed. "I guess we both have secrets. I accept, Harry."

He eyed her strangely. "Accept what?"

"Your offer of friendship. I think we both need a friend. You listen to me and I'll listen to you. Maybe we can help each other. Agreed?" She offered him her hand.

Harry studied her face for a long moment before taking her hand. "Agreed."

Chapter 8

shley smiled as Harry helped her climb out of the truck. There seemed to be a lot of people at the company picnic. "I didn't know this was going to be such a big event. Am I dressed okay?" She wore blue jean shorts and a red flannel shirt over her pink cami.

Harry's expression melted her heart. "Princess, you could be dressed in rags and would still be the most beautiful girl in the world." He stole a quick kiss.

His sister Margaret ran over. "Ash. I love your outfit. How's my future sister-in-law?"

Ashley's mouth dropped open. *What? How did she know?*

Harry's face was blushing as he leaned in. "I may have told Maggot that if it's the last thing I do, I'm going to marry you someday."

Margaret nodded. "And I may have told him he better not wait too long. He needs to do it before everyone else sees how wonderful you are."

Ashley felt her cheeks heat. "Does that mean you like me?"

Margaret swallowed her in a hug. "If I could pick any woman as my sister-in-law, and Harry's wife, it would be you."

"W-why?"

Margaret held her hand and pointed at Harry. "See my brother? He's never been happier. You've brought out the best in him." She turned to Ashley. "And even if that wasn't the case, you're a very special woman. I'm so glad he was lucky enough to find you."

"I-I, uh, don't know what to say."

Margaret shot her a devious wink. "Just say yes when he asks. If you don't, he'll be intolerable."

After Margaret left, Ashley turned to study Harry's smiling face. "You know the answer will be yes, don't you?"

He kissed her deeply. "Yes, I do."

She tagged along with Harry as he finalized a few things. Ashley's pulse raced as Harry introduced her to everyone they met. Her head was spinning as she tried to remember names and faces.

Harry had excused himself to use the restroom. A man approached her. He gave her a curious look. He was shorter than both Harry and Henry, but it was obvious he was their brother. *Edmund.* He carried the air of self-confidence.

"So you must be the girl everyone is talking about. Name's Ashley, right?"

Ellie and Sophie had warned her about him and the sibling rivalry between the brothers. She extended her hand. "Yes. I'm Ashley Snyder. And you're Edmund?"

He raised his eyebrows as he took her hand. He kissed her fingertips and continued to kiss up her arm. "That I am."

Ashley pushed his head away. "I've heard about you."

Edmund laughed. "All good things, I hope. After all, I am the gem of this family." His eyes roved over her body, stopping at the top of her cami.

"Only in your own mind, brother." Harry appeared behind him and walked to Ashley's side. He reached for Ashley's hand. She quickly took it.

She noted the glimmer of something in Edmund's eye. *Anger or hatred?* "Why Harry, this isn't the girl you were holding hands with this morning. Who was it?" Edmund put his finger against his chin and stared into space. His face brightened as he turned to confront his brother. "That's right. You were holding hands with Sophia, weren't you? Wait! Isn't she married to Ben?"

Harry's fingers trembled against hers. Fortunately, Harry had told her about his earlier encounter with Edmund and correctly predicted Edmund would use it as a way to try to cause trouble. *Not to my Harry, you don't.* Ashley got in his face. "Are you talking about when you arrived late to help and walked in on Sophie and Harry talking?"

"So that's what he told you, huh?" The younger brother was quick on his feet. "Looked pretty intimate to me."

Harry took a step forward. Edmund's eyes grew large. Ashley touched Harry's shoulder. "He's not worth it, Harry. I believe you." She turned to face

Edmund. "Think what you want. Harry told me about what happened. We share everything."

Edmund laughed. "You do? Did he tell you he had a crush on my girl?"

Okay. This Edmund jerk was officially annoying. Ashley poked her finger in his chest. "Tara? Yes, he told me. So what?"

Edmund gave her a strange look. "Did he tell you *everything*?"

Troublemaker. "He most certainly did. Can I ask you a personal question, Edmund?"

He winked at her. "Sure."

"Are you adopted?"

Edmund did a double take. "No. Why would you ask that?"

Ashley bit her lip to keep from laughing. "I was just thinking, everyone else in this family is so nice. But you? You're a piece of work, not to mention a jerk."

She squeezed Harry's hand as she spun and walked away. When they rounded the corner of the barn, she turned to him. Harry was staring at her with a look of wonder.

"How'd I do?"

A smile slowly filled his face. "I can't believe it. Put him in his place. Like I always wanted to do, but I'm never quick enough."

Ashley kissed his hand. "Ellie warned me about him. How he always tries to make a fool of you. I won't let him do that. She coached me on what to say." A bad thought ran through her mind. "Did I go too far? Did I upset you?"

Harry framed her face with his hands. "No, but you surprised me. I never thought you'd be that brave, that strong. You're full of surprises."

Ashley wrapped her arms around his neck. "We're not just a couple. You and I, we're a team. I won't let anyone be mean to my king. I love you."

"I love you, too." Harry's lips met hers.

Ashley winked at him. "Whatcha say we see what other trouble we can get into?"

***

Edmund smarted over Ashley's rebuke. But that wasn't all. Ashley was beautiful, maybe the prettiest girl he'd ever met. He was smitten. No wonder old Harry was attracted to her. Oh, he'd overheard the women talking about the pair. How Harry planned to ask Ashley to marry him. But he hadn't yet. Ashley was still fair game. And even if she wasn't, there was nothing Edmund couldn't take away from his older brother. *I'm irresistible.*

Sam Espenshade, one of the employees, grabbed his shoulder. "Edmund. Long time, no see. Whatcha been up to?"

He shifted slightly so he could keep an eye on Ashley and Harry. "Been busy. I work for a painting company now."

Sam eyed him strangely. "Didn't you like working on the farm?"

Edmund let out a dismissive laugh. "Working under the thumb of Henry, the great white warrior, and Harry, the perfect brother? I think not."

Sam shook his head. "Your brothers are the coolest people I've ever met. Really nice. I like working for them."

Ashley and Harry had disappeared around the corner of the big Celebration barn. *Time to move.* "They put on a good front. You don't know what it's like to have to live with them. Nice seeing you again, Sam."

Edmund hurried around the corner, but the pair were nowhere in sight. *Where'd you take her?*

The sudden growl of a diesel engine startled him. It was coming from the back of the barn. Edmund headed that way, yearning to catch another glance of Harry's little honey. He was almost to the corner when the old John Deere appeared in front of him, pulling a hay wagon. Harry was driving and the hottie was sitting on the fender, laughing. Edmund knew Harry wasn't watching, so he quickly moved directly in the path. At the last minute, Harry glanced his way and slammed on the brakes.

"Watch where you're going, you big idiot." Edmund smiled inside when Harry's face turned red.

"What were you doing there?"

"Don't blame this on me. If you'd been paying attention to where you were going instead of her, you'd have seen me."

Harry's hands turned white as he gripped the wheel.

Ashley's voice was firm. "He tried it, Harry. I saw him run in front of you. Ignore him. We have a hay ride to give."

Harry didn't verbalize, but Harry's expression said everything as Edmund headed toward the front of the barn.

***

Ashley proudly rode on the fender as Harry drove the loaded hay wagon around the farm. Harry puttered along and reached for her hand. Ashley proudly took it. *Love your touch, Harry.* There were a number of young women in the wagon who worked for the family. Ashley couldn't help but giggle at the way they looked on with envy at her and her king.

After the last ride, Harry quickly dismounted and reached for her. He softly gripped her hips and started to lift her to the ground. Before she reached the grass, Ashley wrapped her arms around his neck and gave him what she hoped was a mind blowing kiss. *I love the way you smell and taste.*

Harry must have liked it because when she pulled her lips away, his mouth quickly sought hers.

A sour voice interrupted them. "Tsk-tsk. You know Mum doesn't approve of such outward displays of affection."

Ashley felt Harry tense in her arms. She came to his rescue. "Your jealousy is showing, Edmund. Maybe Mum doesn't approve of *your* public displays, but every time Harry kisses me when she's around, she smiles." Edmund's mouth dropped open. Ashley laughed and Harry joined in.

Harry squeezed her hand. "Come on, princess. It's time for lunch."

Over the next twenty minutes, Harry introduced her to everyone they met, *as his girlfriend!*

Sophie appeared and hugged her. "Ashley, so good to see you. Harry been treating you alright? If not, tell me and I'll set the old bugger straight."

She glanced at Harry who was smiling. "Yes. He treats me like royalty."

Sophie winked at Harry. "He'd better. See you around."

From across the barn, Harry's mother suddenly let out a yell and made a bee line straight for her. Darcy crushed her in her arms. "My Ashley. Harry doesn't bring you around often enough for me." When Darcy released her, Ashley's head was spinning. Darcy pinched her in the arm. "Too skinny. You best eat up today. Need to fatten you up a little before..." Her voice trailed away.

The world was starting to come back into focus. "Before what?"

"Come on, lass. I may be old, but I know what's going on. I won't have a skinny daughter-in-law in the family."

Ashley's mouth dropped open and she turned to Harry. His face was red. "What have you been telling everyone?"

He squeezed her hands. "How much I love you and I want you to be my, my..."

She whispered in response. "Wife?"

"Yes," exclaimed Darcy as she walked away.

Harry's kisses consumed her. "Forever and ever. Until time passes away."

Before she could respond, Henry called for everyone's attention. "Thank you all for coming. As usual, my mother has outdone herself. We wanted to cater the meal, but she wouldn't hear of it. Now before we partake, Amos Lapp would like to say grace." The Amish gentleman gave a wonderful blessing, thanking God for everything from the food to the people who ran the company. As soon as he finished, people began lining up at the serving table.

Harry extended his hand to Ashley and led her to the front of the line. He didn't get his food then, but escorted her. The meal was very different than Ashley expected for a picnic. Darcy Campbell had made lamb stew, beef and kidney pie, honey roasted ham, turkey and about fifteen other dishes.

He walked Ashley back to a table and introduced her to a new employee, Hannah Rutledge and her daughters. As Harry walked away, Ashley noted how Hannah looked after him. *Not a chance, sister. He's mine.*

Hands suddenly covered her eyes. "Guess who?"

Ashley knew that voice. *Sam Espenshade.* She hadn't seen him in a while, but she knew him well. He and his sister had visited and sat with her during the dark days of her treatments. She jumped up and hugged him.

"What are you doing here?"

His smile was ear to ear. Sam pulled back but kept his arms around her waist. "I work here. You look great and happy. You work here, too?"

Before he could answer, Harry reappeared with his plate and growled at Sam. Harry's face was bright red. "Get your hands off my girlfriend, right now, or I'll rip off your arm and beat you to death with it."

Sam's face paled as he backed away. "Sorry, boss. I didn't know. Ashley and me, well..."

Ashley was astonished at Harry's jealousy. "Harry! Stop it. Sam is one of my oldest and dearest friends. He used to sit with me after I came back from chemo. He shaved his head when I lost my hair."

Harry's face softened. Harry extended his hand to Sam. "Sorry. Misunderstood. Thank you for being kind to my princess." They sat together, but while Sam engaged in conversation with Ashley and Harry, his eyes were on the other woman, Hannah. The conversation ended when Henry got up to speak.

"Hey, everyone. May I have your attention? I'd like to thank all of you for joining us today at our picnic. It's great to see so many families here today. Ellie, Margaret, Harry and I would like to take a moment to express how glad and blessed we are to have each of you here working with us, as well as taking time out of your lives to bring your families to our home. As a small expression of our thanks, there are gift bags in the rear of the barn. When you leave, take a couple. Now, if we can get a hand from everyone in cleaning up the meal, we'll get on with the fun festivities we've planned. You are welcome to do what you please, but since it's so hot out today, we've decided to divide the barn down the center. Anyone seen Harry?"

Harry stood and waved to his brother.

Henry laughed. "Should have guessed he'd be hanging around Ashley. In case you didn't know, she's his girlfriend."

Ashley knew she was beaming with pride, but Harry turned at least eleven shades of red. Clapping started, as well as many whistles.

Henry waited until the noise settled. "Harry has been gracious enough to find us a couple of thousand fuzzy snowballs, so anyone who wants to join in for Lancaster County's biggest indoor snowball fight, feel free to participate. We also have a karaoke machine for those who want to display their singing skills. We'll be ready for the music to start in just a few minutes. My beautiful wife, Ellie, and her lovely best friend, Sophie, have been practicing. They twisted my bad arm to allow them to go first."

Ashley didn't understand the joke, but everyone laughed. Harry must have seen her confusion. He whispered, "I'll explain later."

Ashley looked over at Ellie, who simply blew Henry a smile-laced kiss. Ellie always glowed whenever Henry was around. *Kind of like me when Harry's near.*

Henry continued. "We thank each and every one of you for making this company what it is. Have a wonderful time and enjoy yourselves."

So many people helped clean up that Ashley couldn't find anything to do. A long curtain was drawn, splitting the barn in two. She followed Harry to a corner of the far side of the building. He walked up to a large box and overturned it. Hundreds if not thousands of white, fluffy balls spilled onto the floor. Many of the kids ran to scoop them up. Harry made off with an armful, hurling them at people. He turned and threw one at Ashley, hitting her in the leg. "Gotcha, princess!"

Ashley laughed. "Oh no, you didn't!" She grabbed several from the floor and gave chase. Harry was laughing as he ran from her, hiding behind people along the way. Ashley tried to hit him, but missed. She found herself out of ammunition.

Music caught her attention. It took her a second to realize the voices belonged to Sophie and Ellie. They were singing that Sonny and Cher song they'd been practicing the day she met them in the Tea Room. She turned to look for Harry when a snowball hit her in the face. Sam streaked by, laughing at her. She continued to take part in the snowball fight, throwing them at both Sam and Harry. In the distance, she saw Harry chasing Sam.

A hand grabbed her arm and pulled her to a secluded spot against the barn wall. *Edmund.* He twisted her arms at each side and pushed them behind her, preventing Ashley from moving. The closeness of his lips against her neck was scary.

The scent of black licorice from his mouth filled her nostrils. Edmund's voice was soft and teasing. "Rumor has it you might become my sister-in-law. A pity, really. Someone as sweet and pretty as you deserves a real man." Edmund's lips touched her neck. "A man who can satisfy your every need." He nibbled on her ear.

"Stop it. Let me go."

He kissed her ear and rubbed his nose against hers. "Why does he call you princess?" Edmund released her arms and placed his hands on her hips. "You must be a gem. Mind if I go treasure hunting?"

Ashley shoved him away. "Keep your filthy hands off of me."

"One kiss and you'll forget him." He took a step toward her.

"Leave now or I'll tell Harry. How do you think he'll react when I tell him you tried to force me to kiss you?"

His smile left for a few seconds before reappearing. "You won't tell him. You liked my lips on your neck."

Ashley's hands were on her hips as she held her ground. "Really? Try me."

"Well, isn't this a predicament?"

"What's a predicament?" Ashley and Edmund both turned toward a red faced Harry.

"What did you do, you little snipe?"

Edmund put his hands in front of him and started backing away from his brother. Harry stepped threateningly toward Edmund.

"It's not what you think..."

"Really?"

Ashley had to stop it. "The predicament was, uh, he just found out you want to marry me and he, uh, um, didn't know how to tell his big brother, uh, how happy he was for us." She directed her eyes towards Edmund. "Isn't that right?"

Edmund's expression of surprise was quickly covered. He nodded and said, "Yes, uh, that's right."

Harry poked his finger into Edmund's chest. "I don't believe that. I know you too well, you good for nothing..." His hand reached for Edmund's neck.

Ashley touched Harry's arm. "Don't believe Edmund. Believe me instead."

Harry stopped and turned to her, softly framing her face with both hands. He kissed her. "I'll always believe you, but watch my brother. He's no good." He turned to face Edmund while he directed his voice at Ashley. "If he ever touches you or makes you feel uncomfortable, just let me know. I'll thrash him within an inch of his life."

The karaoke song ended. Ashley heard Ellie dedicate the next song to her love, her Henry. She stopped and listened while Ellie sang the words to *Moonlight Serenade.* Her voice was beautiful and very melodic. She whispered to Harry, "Dance with me."

Her king turned and held her in his arms. He was clumsy, but his embrace felt so good around her. Edmund was forgotten as the two stumbled together.

Everything was wonderful until Ellie's voice stopped and she gave a sudden cry. It sounded like pain and desperation. "Henry, please come here. I need you."

Harry grabbed Ashley's hand and pulled her along with him to the other side of the curtain. *What's happening?* Ellie was kneeling on the improvised stage, holding her belly. The immediate family had run to her side, but Henry called for everyone to back away and give her room.

Ashley's heart was in her throat as she tried to figure out what had happened. From a distance, she could see Henry was speaking on his cell phone. The entire barn became quiet as everyone gathered round. Ashley heard people around her murmuring. It dawned on her they were praying for Ellie.

Ashley's vision blurred as she watched Sophie hold her friend's hand. Sophie was crying. Ashley noted Darcy and Margaret wringing their hands and leaning on each other. Some of the men and women around her started praying loudly. She whispered to Harry, "What's going on? What happened?"

"I don't know. Wish there was something we could do. I pray to God Ellie's all right."

Suddenly, Henry grabbed the karaoke machine's microphone. "Ladies and gentlemen, might be time for our daughter to join us. We're leaving for the hospital. Stay as long as you like and enjoy yourselves. Hopefully the next time I see you, I'll show you pictures of our little Maggie May. Ta-ta, everyone."

Ashley turned to Harry. "She's having her baby?"

He was beaming. "She might be."

"Can we go see the baby in the hospital?"

Henry motioned to his brother. Harry ran to him, but immediately returned to Ashley. His voice had an urgency. "Lend me a hand. Henry asked me to get a few things. They didn't pack yet." Without waiting for a response, he literally dragged her along. They ran to the sprawling home of Ellie and Henry. Bounding up the stairs, Harry instructed her to go through Ellie's dresser drawers to get things for her. Ashley wasn't comfortable rummaging through Ellie's undergarments, but did. Harry ran out of the room, reappearing with a suitcase. Together, they stuffed the clothes inside.

They ran outside just as Henry was finishing strapping Ellie into the car. When Henry moved out of the way, Harry fell to his knees, kissing and hugging Ellie. Henry grabbed the suitcase and flung it in the rear seat of their car. By now, everyone was outside to wave goodbye as the car drove off.

Harry turned to Ashley, excitement overflowing. "I'm going to be an uncle and you, an aunt."

Chapter 9

Ellie was exhausted, but Henry had never seen a more wonderful sight than his *two* girls. He sat on the edge of the bed, holding little Margaret May Campbell. Though almost two weeks early, she weighed in at six pounds, nine and one-quarter ounces. Maggie appeared to have her priorities in line because the first thing she wanted to do was nurse.

Henry and Ellie murmured in amazement at how perfect their little girl was. Her brown eyes, black hair, ten toes and ten fingers thrilled them beyond expression. As Ellie nursed her firstborn, Henry offered a prayer of thanks for both of the little ladies.

"Ellie, do you know you are the most beautiful woman I have ever seen?"

She replied with a tired smile. "Sweetheart, you always say that, even when I'm at my worst."

He grinned. "I've never seen you not at your best. You're always beautiful to me."

"Yes, you have. Remember when you woke up in the hospital, right after you rescued me? I looked awful that day. Two black eyes, cuts and bruises, a bandage on my lip and badly in need of a haircut. How in the world could I have looked beautiful that day?"

Henry remembered. "Even then, I knew there was no one else nearly as beautiful as you are to me. I love you so much."

They kissed, long and soft, until Maggie started to cry. Daddy picked her up, softly patting her back so she could burp.

The nurse slipped in. "How are we doing?" Ellie offered a soft and tired smile. "Great. There's a crowd of people in the waiting room who've been here since yesterday. They, as the one man put it, 'demand an audience with Queen Ellie and Princess Margaret'."

Henry looked at Ellie, who nodded. Henry bowed to the nurse. "Bring in my lady's subjects." The woman disappeared and Henry turned to give his wife a final kiss before bedlam ensued.

Darcy was the first one through the door, arms outstretched toward little Maggie. A wide smile filled her face. "My wee one." The entire extended family was there, Edmund and Tara, Harry and Ashley, Margaret, Ben and Sophie and even Susan Miller. For the next twenty minutes, they passed Maggie around while hugging and kissing Henry's family.

The nurse came in. "Mommy and Daddy need rest. Everyone else, out." After they left, she wheeled in a small cot for Henry to sleep on. He kissed Ellie one last time before he took his place next to her, holding her hand. He knew Ellie was hungry, but she needed sleep above all else.

***

Ben and Sophie held it together until they entered their car. Ben cradled his wife as they cried. The long discussions and arguments about adoption or artificial insemination were things of the past. Holding little Maggie had settled his mind. Sophie wanted Henry to be the donor. Ben wanted anyone but Henry to be the donor. That had been the constant argument. Ben wasn't crying out of self-pity, but because he couldn't give Sophie what she wanted most, a child. He clung to his wife.

Sophie was the first to speak. "I concede. I wanted Henry to be the father because of his genes and his personality, not because he's Henry. I could sense as you held that little girl, you want to be a daddy. I won't press the point anymore. Pick whoever you want, but it's time to have a baby." Her face was wet.

Ben wiped his cheeks. What price was she paying, giving in to his wishes? As much as it bothered him that she wanted Henry to provide the seed, he knew what he needed to do. He held Sophie's head between his hands, looking into her beautiful Italian eyes. "Soph, when I saw you holding her, I knew what you wanted. I'll need God's help to deal with this, but if you want Henry to be the donor, I'll agree."

Sophie's jaw dropped and she looked at him in disbelief. "What? Why would you change your mind?"

He kissed her hand. "Before I answer that, tell me something. You've never once asked me for anything, never forced me or played games with our love. Even when I almost let how I felt about Ellie come between us, you never pushed the issue. Why was that?"

Her eyes welled. "Because I love you and when you love someone, you never put that at risk. I'll never force you to do anything. When it came down to Ellie or me, I prayed you'd choose me. Love, or anything else that you make someone feel isn't love. I wanted your love freely given. That's why."

Ben grabbed her, squeezing her body tightly against him. "I love you so much. You're the perfect woman, and I'm not talking about your beautiful body or pretty face. It's what's inside of you that's perfect. We both want a child. I don't fully understand why, but I know you want Henry to be the donor. I'll be okay with that. I hope you realize how much I love you."

Sophie held him tightly. "Thank you. I'll never ask for anything again."

***

Edmund was whistling a Taylor Swift song as they drove back to Tara's home. Tara had been quiet since they left the hospital. Something was on her mind and Edmund knew exactly what it was. That's why he was whistling. Edmund didn't want to have the conversation Tara desired. He still wasn't sure about her, or their future, especially after meeting Ashley.

He pulled up in front of her garage, turned off the engine and started to get out. Tara put her hand on his arm. "Can we talk for a moment?"

Great. Here it comes. He glanced at her, trying to figure a way to avoid this talk. "I'm pretty tired. Long night. Let's catch a quick nap first."

She stared at him. Edmund suddenly felt naked and exposed under her gaze. Holding Maggie had stirred something in Tara. This had been building for a long time. "Maggie's beautiful, isn't she?"

Edmund swallowed, hard. "Yes. Resembles her mother, don't you think?"

"She does." He could sense the bomb dropping before it hit. "Do you want children?"

Boom. "Maybe, eventually, I don't know. We're still early in our romance. I don't think now's the time to discuss this. How about that nap?" He looked away from her.

Tara gently grasped his chin and turned him until their eyes met. "Where are we going in our relationship? Do you love me or is this all a matter of convenience?"

He was starting to sweat. He restarted the car and maximized the air conditioning. This was going to be tougher than he'd thought. "Of course I love you. Don't I show you enough?"

She hesitated. "I guess, but I want more than what we have. Tell me your dreams and plans for us. Do you plan on marrying me and starting a family anytime soon?"

There it was. He'd known sooner or later, she'd broach this subject. "Yes, someday, but it's way too soon to even consider either marriage or children, don't you think? I mean, we talked about travelling and seeing the world. Those things should come first."

She wiped her eyes. *Don't cry, woman. Can't stomach that.*

Tara looked away. "We discussed those things, but I'm ready for the future. Do you ever plan on marrying me?"

He'd almost made up his mind, until yesterday. Meeting Ashley had stirred something very passionate in his soul. Having to sit across from Harry, seeing him hold that girl's hand had been painful. *I thought I loved Tara, but...* Edmund masked his feelings. "I do, but I was, I was kind of enjoying being us right now. Is there a need to rush things?"

Tara sniffed hard. "I understand. This is a great relationship for you, but I don't think you really love me."

"No. I do love you." *I like things the way they are.* "I can't see me living life without you." *Unless it's with Ashley?* He shook his head to clear the thought. Guilt filled him. *You deserve more than I've given you.* He reached for her hands. "You're special. Why do you love me? Maybe that's the better question."

Her face softened and she touched his cheek. "I love you just because you're you. Your voice, your spirit, the feeling inside me when I'm with you. You're my every dream come true. That's why. Why do you love me?"

Do I love her? As he studied her eyes, his thoughts ran rampant. There were many things about Tara that annoyed him, yet for every negative, there were ten positives. "I love you, just because."

"Because of what?"

"A zillion reasons."

Tara's face lit up. "Yeah? What's your favorite thing about me?"

"The taste of your kisses in the morning."

Her eyebrows raised. "Go on."

"The touch of your hand in mine."

"Anything else?"

"The way you feel in my arms."

Tara shook her head and looked away.

"Did I say something wrong?"

She focused on something outside the window. "No."

"What's going on?"

She rapidly turned to face him. "I can't wait any longer. I want commitment and I want it now."

It wasn't so much her words, but the way she'd said them. Like he owed it to her. "And if I don't want that now?"

Tara shook her head. "You take me for granted."

Edmund's anger spiraled skyward. *This is about control.* "Take you for granted? No, It's the other way around. You are aware I can have any woman I want, aren't you? But I'm with you."

Her eyes flashed fire. "Well, thank you for stooping into the gutter to pick despicable little me. I'm such a lucky girl." Tara turned away from him. Some time elapsed before she spoke again. "You aren't the only one with options. I need to think this through."

Things were going the wrong way. "I didn't mean to be insensitive. Let's start over."

Tara nodded. "Okay. I liked your idea about a nap. I'm going to head in."

That was way *too easy.* "Good. I'm looking forward to cuddling with you."

She opened the car door. "Alone."

He grabbed her hand. "By yourself?"

She pulled out of his grasp and looked toward, but not at him. "That's the definition of alone."

"I don't understand. We always..."

Tara cut him off. "Not today. You stay outside. See you later."

Edmund was flabbergasted. "Okay. Remember I love you."

She stared at him for a while before responding, "Thanks." The sound of the door closing was like the end of the world.

What just happened?

***

Harry held her hand as they walked to the parking garage. It took everything Ashley had not to lose control. The way Harry glowed when he held the infant. *Not fair to him. I need to stop this, now.*

After they were seated in the truck, Ashley's blurry eyes stared aimlessly out the window. Harry softly touched her hair.

"What's wrong, princess?"

"Don't call me that anymore." She couldn't look at him.

He touched her arm. "What's the matter?"

"Let's go somewhere, far away and talk."

She could hear the change in his voice. "Okay, but we could talk now."

"No. I need time." *And courage.*

They rode in silence. Harry navigated out of the city and turned west on the interstate. He got off at Columbia and headed north on one of the state roads. Just over the crest, he pulled into a lot. She quickly exited so he couldn't open the door for her. Her heart was breaking in two.

Harry caught up and framed her face with his hands. "You're crying. What did I do?"

"Nothing. Let's find someplace quiet. We need to talk."

Harry walked back to the truck, grabbed a backpack and offered his arm. Ashley stepped away without taking it and headed up the trail. Harry followed. At a clearing overlooking the Susquehanna River, she sat on a bench. She couldn't help it. Her sorrow overflowed into her hands. Harry wrapped his arms around her and pulled her close. *This is so hard, ending us. I wish...*

Harry was patient, waiting for her to speak. Finally, she dried her eyes. "I d-don't th-think it's a good idea for us to see each other anymore."

Harry let go and knelt in front of her. *Can't look at you.* Ashley directed her gaze across the Susquehanna River to York County. He cleared his throat. She turned and stared into his eyes. He was smiling. Harry had seen right through her lie.

"Why?"

The scent of cut grass almost took her breath away when she sniffled. "Because, I, uh, don't l-l-love you anymore."

Harry touched her face gently. "Nonsense. What is this about?"

Her vision grew blurry as she studied him. *Everything I ever wanted...* So royal, so handsome. *My every dream.* "I, I just don't want to see you anymore. It's best that we break up."

The firmness of his voice startled her. "No. Not until you tell me the truth. I love you, Ashley. You at least owe me the courtesy of telling me why."

She tried to stand, but Harry warmly grasped her arms. "Talk to me, please? I love you."

Ashley put her head back, noting the vapor trails of a jet marking the clear blue sky. *Even people flying from New York to L.A. can see his love.*

"I'm just not the girl for you. I can't give you what you want or need."

"Why would you even think that?"

"Because..." Harry was patient, waiting for her to continue. His gaze made her squirm. "B-because I saw how you looked when you held Maggie. You want children, Harry, and I can't, I can't..." Ashley broke down.

Harry engulfed her in his arms, patting her back. "It'll be fine. I know, princess. I know."

She pushed him away. "Know what?"

"What the cancer did to your body. You can't have children. It's alright, I don't care. I love you, just the way you are."

How could you know? "I don't understand. How did you find out?"

Harry kissed her lips ever so sweetly. "Your mom told me."

"What? When?"

"When you were sick. Your mother and I had a long talk. I asked her and she told me everything."

Her world was spinning. *I still don't understand.* "Asked her what?"

He reached into the book bag. "I asked her if I could marry you and after I slew every doubt she had, your mother said yes." Harry opened a ring box. The summer sun set the gem on fire before her eyes. It was dazzling. "I hope you'll say yes."

It was hard to get her breath. "But I can't give you children."

"So?" He brushed her hair from her eyes and kindly wiped away her tears. "I love you, because you are you, not because of your ability to have children. I want to spend my life with you. You alone. Will you marry me, princess?"

This is what I wanted, until... "But I saw the joy in your eyes ... how much you loved holding that little girl. That will never be us."

His smile was melting her resolve. "I don't care. If we, you and I together, decide we want a child someday, we'll adopt. If not, it doesn't matter. I love you. Will you marry me?"

"B-but what if..."

Harry's finger brushed her lips. "Always and forever. It won't matter. I'll be right by your side. And nothing will come between us. Never, ever. You and I, always."

"Harry, suppose..."

"Ashley. I'm kneeling in front of you. You can't deny we were meant to be."

"No, but you want kids and..."

"Princess, listen to me. I want you more than kids or everything else in the world. Any decision about adopting or not adopting, we'll make together. This isn't about me. It's about us. I love you and you love me, don't you?"

Yes, yes. "Sorry I lied..."

Nothing but understanding was on his face. "I saw right through it. You were being brave, trying to protect me." His lips found hers again. "Please close your eyes for a second. I want to show you something."

Ashley wiped her cheeks again before closing her eyes. The sound of a train engine drifted up the hill from the tracks along the river. Harry's hands softly touched both sides of her head.

"There. Open your eyes, princess."

Ashley's eyes involuntarily widened at the sight before her. Her hand flew to her head. *Our teapot crowns!* Amazement. "Harry..."

Harry's smile destroyed all doubts. "Princess, your king asks the honor of joining his life with yours, evermore. Will you marry me?"

Ashley drew a deep breath. Stepping forward would be like jumping off a cliff, with him. *My dreams are right before me.* She leapt forward. "Yes. Can't wait to marry you, you old pot head."

Chapter 10

*T*he chill of the air conditioning sent a shiver up Tara's spine. Crawling out of the bed, she made her way to the bathroom. *Not much of a nap.* Her mind had replayed the conversation with Edmund. Everything he'd said about why he loved her had been physical reasons. *If he does love me, it's not because of what's inside me.*

After a warm shower, she studied herself in the mirror. Time was starting to make its mark. Her hair lacked the luster it once had. Crow's feet were making an appearance around her eyes. That didn't even cover the physical evidence time was taking on her body. *Life's passing me by.*

She dressed in shorts and a light colored linen top. She needed to find Edmund. It was time to find out where this relationship was going, *if anywhere at all.* Tara reached in her purse to retrieve her cell to call him, but when she dialed, his ringtone resonated in her purse. *That's right.* Earlier at the hospital, Edmund had given her his phone for safe keeping.

Instead of driving over to return it, she covered the short distance between the houses on foot. Now was as good as any time to get the issue out in the open. In the late afternoon sun, the mirage of glistening water on the road caught her eye before it disappeared. *Just like my dreams, fading away.* Tara wiped sweat from her brow. The coolness would feel good inside the Campbell's house.

Happy faces of pansies greeted her as she walked up to the porch. Just a few seconds after she knocked, Margaret opened the door. She was beaming. "Tara. What a treat. Come in where it's comfortable. Get you some tea? Mum made iced cranberry hibiscus. How 'bout I pour you a glass?"

Margaret was always so kind to her. "Splendid. Did you get a nap?"

Margaret's sleepy smile said more than her words. Little Maggie had been long anticipated. "Not yet. Too excited."

Thick arms wrapped themselves around her. Darcy kissed her cheek. "Nice to see you, child. What did you think of my first grandbaby?"

Hello to you, too, Mum. Darcy didn't have to enunciate the hint. She'd made it plain, over and over, that she wanted lots of grandchildren and hoped Tara would help the cause. *Will that ever happen?* Before Tara could respond, the door swung open. Harry and Ashley poured in, laughing. She'd never seen the big man look so happy.

"Mum, Maggot, Tara. We've got splendid news!"

Darcy's hand trembled against Tara's shoulder. "What is it?"

Ashley thrust her left hand out, displaying the glistening stone on her finger. "Check this out! Harry proposed and I said yes!" The little blonde danced as she sang the next words. "We're getting married. We're getting married."

Darcy and Margaret ran to engulf Ashley in joyful embraces. If Harry smiled any wider, his teeth would surely fall out. But despite the happiness in the room, a coldness filled Tara's soul. *I've done my time. That should be me... and Edmund.*

Harry stumbled over and ripped Tara off her stool, holding her tightly in his arms. "I'm so glad you're here. Thanks for celebrating with us." The feel of his lips so close to her ear stirred a memory. She was suddenly back at Ellie and Henry's wedding, in Harry's embrace. He'd trembled when he held her that night. She'd sensed the deep affection Harry had for her, but Edmund swept her away. Harry's hands weren't trembling for her now. His exuberance flowed in every direction like a shock wave, because of Ashley.

When he released her, Tara had to grab the stool to keep from falling. *I chose the wrong brother.* In those few seconds, his touch moved her. The love flowing out of Harry was so real, she could almost touch it. *Why couldn't that be me?* If he ever proposed, Edmund's reaction surely wouldn't be the same as Harry's.

Harry turned his attention to his intended, leading her into the living room. Darcy and Margaret followed, leaving Tara alone with her thoughts. The electricity between the loving couple still hung in the air. There was no doubt they were in love. Tara's mind raced between Edmund and Harry. *If I'd picked Harry, would that be me now?* It wasn't right. Everything Tara wanted, had cultivated and tried to build with Edmund, now belonged to Ashley and Harry. And it had happened so quickly. *Life's not fair. Why can't I have what I want?*

A quiet voice whispered to her soul. *Edmund doesn't love you. He only loves what you do.*

She whispered to herself. "No, that can't be true."

Her breath refused to come. The world grew blurry.

A thought formed inside her, calming her with icy cold tendrils. *Really? Put him to the test. Time will tell the truth.* Tara shook her head to clear the thought. She drained the glass of fuchsia colored liquid.

In the next room, happiness and love were abounding, but standing alone in the kitchen, only bitter disappointment surrounded her. She placed Edmund's phone on the counter and stepped outside. Her eyes studied the sky. A lone dove flew away from her, only to be joined by its mate further down the road. They spread their wings toward the horizon. Far away and together they flew. Tara's footsteps followed.

***

Edmund had spent the afternoon walking around the farm. *Why'd Harry have to find her, now?* He knew what he should do, ask Tara to marry him, but the way Ashley made him feel... He stood outside Tara's house for a long time before realizing her car was gone. *Today sucks.*

It was after dark when he walked into the home he shared with his family. Margaret and Darcy were laughing in the kitchen, drinking wine.

Margaret's smile was unending. "Edmund, come have a glass. We're celebrating."

He sat at the table and his sister filled a goblet with a light yellow liquid. He raised his glass. "To little Maggie May."

Darcy's words stopped his toast in mid-air. "And my new daughter."

"I think you mean grand-daughter."

He'd never seen his mother look so happy. "To both of them."

The wine spilled out of his shaking hand. "What do you mean, both of them?"

Margaret hiccupped and covered her mouth. "I don't think he knows, Mum."

Edmund's lack of sleep contributed to his confusion. "Don't know what?"

Margaret stood, smiling down on him. "You and I, brother, now have another sister in the family. Harry proposed and Ashley accepted. They're getting married."

Chills cascaded down his spine. If Tara found out, she'd be so upset. His girl had been hinting about tying the knot for months. *And I dragged my feet... for too long.* He stood, eyes flipping back and forth between the women. Words tumbled out of his mouth, ones he meant to keep under his breath. "Damn you, Harry."

Darcy's face clouded. "What'd you say?"

"Uh, darned good, Harry."

Margaret shook her head. "Not what I heard. You're miffed because he beat you to the punch. Should have asked Tara first, now, shouldn't you?"

His mother chimed in. "Shoulda' married her two years ago. Coulda' had the first grandchild."

He turned away without answering. He needed to see Tara now. Might still be time to ask her before she found out. *Wait, she's not home.* He reached into his pockets for his phone, suddenly remembering he'd asked Tara to hold it. *Now what?*

A whistling noise filled his ears. My phone? He glanced and there it was. Sitting on the counter. "How, how'd my phone get here?"

Darcy answered. "Isn't that where you left it?"

"N-no. Tara had it."

"Maybe she dropped it off when she was here."

His mouth went dry. "T-T-Tara was here? When?"

"Couple hours ago. When Harry and his bride-to-be stopped by to tell us the news."

He couldn't control his breathing. "What'd she say?"

Darcy and Margaret shared a look before shrugging. His sister answered. "Dunno. She must've left while we were in with Harry. Have you spoken with her?" Edmund shook his head. "Try calling her."

He retrieved his phone and saw the text message waiting – from Tara.

Don't know if you're aware, but Harry proposed to Ash. I need some time to think about everything. Don't call or come to see me for a while. We'll need to talk. Plan on a discussion in four weeks. That should be enough time.

Edmund collapsed onto the stool, then muttered, "I've done it this time."

***

The grand opening of the tea room would be on Saturday. For the first time in a long while, Sophie's heart was filled with joy. Now that she and Benjy were on the same page about asking Henry. But the timing had to be just right.

The door swung open. Ashley waltzed in, followed by Harry. They looked so happy.

"Morning, Soph. I'll give you a hand as soon as I say goodbye to Harry." Ashley turned and wrapped her arms around Harry's head. In return, Harry engulfed her.

Sophie smiled. "I'll brew us a spot of tea while you two..." It was no sense continuing. They were ignoring her. *Just like Benjy and me.*

Ashley bounced into the brew room. "Got something to ask you."

She turned to her friend. "What's that?"

"Will you be my co-maid of honor?"

"I'm sorry. Did you say co-maid?"

"Yep. You and Ellie. You two are the reason we fell in love."

Sophie laughed. "I'd be delighted, but somehow, I don't think we can take any credit."

Before Ashley could speak, the bell on the shop door rang. Sophie stepped out to see Edmund walk in. He held his ball cap in his hand. "Morning,

Sophie." Ashley walked to stand next to her. "How are you, Ashley?" he asked.

"I'm fine."

"Good. Sophie, can I speak with you, privately?"

Ashley turned to walk back into the brew room. "I'll work on filling the bottles that came yesterday."

"Thanks. Have a seat, Edmund. Want some tea?" He shook his head.

Edmund looked sad. Tara had told her what happened. Sophie didn't know whether to be angry with, or feel bad for him. "What's up?"

His eyes didn't meet hers. "I'm sure Tara told you what happened." Sophie nodded. "How is she?"

"Surviving."

"When you see her, give her my best." He turned his gaze to look directly into her eyes. "I know you don't like me, and frankly, I understand why. The last two weeks have made me reconsider a lot of things. Mainly how I've treated your sister-in-law. I don't expect you to believe me, but I've changed inside. I plan on making it up to Tara. Now, don't say anything to her, but I do ask you and Ben to reconsider how I've acted versus the way I'll behave from this point forward."

The clip clop of a buggy passing on the road briefly caught his attention. When he returned his gaze to her, his eyes were watery. "I've made a mess of things, not only with her, but with my family. I'm working hard to change that. I'm trying to make amends with Harry and I asked Henry to hire me back. Making a fresh start."

"Why tell me?"

"Because, if God allows, we might be related, hopefully."

Her mouth fell open. "Does that mean..."

"Yes, I plan on asking Tara for her hand. Please forgive me for how I've acted. I can't go back and undo things, but I plan on acting like I should from now on. You mean the world to Tara and I wanted you to know."

She reached out and touched his hand. His was trembling. "I don't quite know what to say."

"Don't say anything. Just please judge me not by my past, but by my future. Mum is planning a big celebration for Ashley and Harry. The same day Tara said we could talk again. If God's willing, I hope to make it an even bigger day." Edmund squeezed her hand, then stood up. He then took a long look toward the store room where Ashley was working, finally looking down and shaking his head. "Give my regards to Ashley. Thanks for giving me your time."

Sophie was speechless as she watched Edmund walk out the door. "Is he serious or is this another of his wild schemes?" Only time would tell.

***

Tara's head pounded. She was having trouble concentrating on the medical chart on the computer. *Edmund.* He'd obeyed her request not to contact her and the withdrawal from not being with him was a killer.

A knock at her door interrupted her thoughts. "Come in."

Tracy, the practice manager, walked in. She carried two cups of coffee from a local convenience store and handed one to Tara. "Got a couple of minutes?"

Tara nodded. "Sure. Anything beats charting." She wrapped her hands around the warm drink.

Tracy laughed. "Pumpkin spice mochas. They're rushing the season a little, but I remembered how much you liked them."

How thoughtful. "Thanks. What's up?"

Tracy pulled up a chair and propped her feet on the desk. "You tell me."

"What do you mean?"

Tracy let out a long sigh. "For the past couple of weeks, you've been moping. What's wrong?"

Tara looked out the window. "Nothing."

"I know you better than that. Spill your guts. Something's up. Is it work or something more important?"

Tara studied the other woman. They didn't run around together, but got along well. Tracy was caring and never gossiped like the rest of the staff. "Not work, but don't worry about it."

Tracy took a long swig and fanned her mouth. "Man, that's hot. Tara, I'm worried about you. Not on a professional level, but a personal one. Despite my position, I care about you. Did something happen?"

Edmund's smile flashed in her mind. Tara's eyes were scratchy. "Yes, but I'm sure you don't have the time for my sob story."

"Try me. Jake took the kids to dinner for some daddy time, so I've got all night. If you need a friend, I'm here for you."

Tara hesitated before responding. "Edmund and I had a fight. Told him I needed some time to think about... us."

"And?"

The dam broke open. For the next twenty minutes, Tara poured out her heart, her fears and her worries. "We've been in this relationship for three years. It's going nowhere. I've come to realize I'm just a convenience, not someone he really loves." She fought to control her emotions, but a sob escaped.

Tracy stood and hugged Tara. "It's okay. Let's figure it out, together."

"I know it's time to break up, but it's so hard. I gave him everything, my heart, my dreams and... well, everything."

"I'm sorry he's such a jerk. You, my friend, need to be happy in life and sometimes we have to move on to find happiness."

"I was happy, with him. He's the only man I ever really loved. Who else would ever love me?"

Tracy brushed Tara's hair from her eyes. "Any man would be lucky to have you. I think we need to build up your self-esteem. Repeat after me, I'm special and lovable and wonderful."

"No, I'm not. Just a plain girl with nothing to offer anyone."

"Yeah, right. You're funny and smart and cool. And pretty on top of everything. Now repeat what I said. I'm special, lovable and any man would be lucky to have me."

"Tracy..."

"I won't give up until you say it."

Tara sniffled. "I'm special."

"And?"

"Funny."

"Keep going."

"And lovable?"

"And any man would be? Say it."

Tara took a sip of the sugary coffee before setting it on the desk. *Too hot to drink.* "I'll only say it to get you to stop. Any man would be lucky to have me. Aw, I don't see how any man—"

Tracy patted Tara's shoulder. "Open your eyes, girl."

"To what?"

"Ever notice the way Dr. Rohrer looks at you?"

"Rohrer? He never says more than 'hi'."

"Right. That's because he respects you and your relationship with the idiot. However, Rohrer's eyes give him away. He likes you, and besides, he's a real nice guy."

He likes me? Really? "I think you're just saying that."

"Hmm. Ever notice he's always working when you are?"

"That's because you schedule it that way."

Tracy giggled. "Pessimist. Look at the schedule and how it's adjusted in pen. He trades with the other docs to be here when you're in the office. And remember the secret Santa gifts you got last year and didn't know who they were from? It was him. Maybe you should take notice. Besides, he's not the only one who likes you."

"You're exaggerating. Who else?"

Tracy shook her head. "That information will cost you. Let's do supper and I'll tell you my point of view. I don't gossip or say much, but I see all. Come on, let's go."

Tara considered the offer. "Oh, what the heck. Where do you want to go?"

"You're buying, but I think Mexican. Time to add a little spice to your life."

Tara dried her eyes with a tissue. Maybe Tracy was right. "Okay, but you're the designated driver. I might need a drink."

"Or two?"

Tara laughed for the first time all day. "Could be three." Maybe it *was* time to explore life outside her own little world.

Chapter 11

Ellie smiled. Life couldn't be going better. Henry's decision to take a couple of weeks off was the best thing to happen to them. They'd always been close, but somehow, they grew closer every day. Henry made it a point to spoil his wife at every opportunity he could. Maggie would soon be three weeks old and Ellie hadn't even had the chance to change her diaper one single time.

Henry walked in, bringing her a cold diet cola. "Hi, honey. Felt you might be thirsty."

He did it again. He read my mind. "How do you do this?" He shot her his million dollar smile and winked. "You know, this ability to read my feelings gives you a wonderful advantage."

His kiss was soft and warm. "Good. Might need it someday, you know, in case I do something stupid."

"Like that would ever happen." She grabbed hold of his shirt and pulled him toward her. "Do you know how much I love you?"

His lips grazed her ear. "Precisely as much as I love you." Henry started nuzzling her neck, but the doorbell rang. He shot her a look of longing. "Better not be another salesman trying to sell us lawn services. I might have to thrash him."

She closed her eyes, relishing in his scent. Okay, he smelled like baby powder these days, but how Henry turned her on. Laughter from the next room interrupted the fantasy forming in her mind.

"Look who I found hanging out on our doorstep." Sophie and Ben were always frequent visitors, but they visited at least once a day since the baby arrived.

Sophie ran to hug Ellie. "You glow, my friend." Sophie glistened. Her best friend had always been emotional, often breaking out into tears, but there was something different in her eyes today. "Is my favorite niece awake?"

"Maggie? Here I thought you came to see me."

The pink on Sophie's cheek betrayed her words. "Of course I did. But since we were in the neighborhood, I wouldn't mind snuggling with your daughter."

Ben walked over and kissed Ellie's cheek. "Ignore her. Of course we came to see you. How's the proud mama?"

The glow the pair both exhibited was significant. *Something happened.* In the last weeks, Ellie had witnessed happiness return to her friend's demeanor. *What is it?* During the last visit, when it was just Ellie and Sophie in the room, her friend whispered she had a very important favor to ask of Ellie. When Henry suddenly returned, she quickly changed the subject. Sophie never found her way back to the topic. Ellie knew her best friend well enough to know that Sophie would circle back around to whatever it was, in due time.

Ben cleared his throat. "Soph and I were wondering if the two of you would like to go out to dinner. That is, if you can trust anyone else to watch Maggie. It'll be our treat. Sophie found this little place in Mount Gretna that's supposed to have great steaks. You guys game on Saturday night?"

Something about the way Ben was fidgeting got her attention. Curiosity filled her mind... not just hers, but Henry's, too. He shot Ellie another wink, which she returned. "I think that would be great. Let's see if we can get a sitter."

A soft cry from the baby monitor caught Ellie's attention. Henry turned toward the nursery, but Sophie interrupted. "May I get her, please?"

"I'll help," Ben offered.

"Okay. Henry, would you mind..."

"Yes, love. I'll get a blanket so you can nurse Maggie." He blew a kiss her way.

Before long, Sophie and Ben reappeared, carrying the little one. Ellie couldn't help but notice the happiness in Sophie's eyes. As Sophie's best friend, she was well aware of the struggles and also the fighting between the couple about having children. *They've reached an agreement.*

Daddy took his daughter in his arms and changed her before passing the infant to Ellie. Henry held the privacy cloth up until Maggie was situated.

Ellie wondered at the way Ben and Sophie smiled as they held hands. "Okay you two, what's going on? Something's up."

An immediate pink color filled Sophie's face. "We've made a monumental decision."

Happiness filled Ellie. "About having children?"

Sophie wrinkled her nose. "Kind of."

"Well, don't keep us in suspense."

The couple searched each other's faces. She caught the slight shake of Ben's head. Sophie was slow in her reply.

"We're, uh, just not ready to share it. Not yet."

That's odd. "Just with us or everyone?"

"With everyone, but especially you two. I promise, you'll be the first to know."

***

Ashley was excited as Harry opened the door for her. Harry told her he had a special surprise tonight. Her bag carried the swimsuit he'd asked her to bring along. A one-piece to cover up the scars. Her first swimsuit since she was six. *Where's he going to take me?* She entered the Campbell house to find Darcy fluffing her graying reddish hair in the mirror. Darcy turned and engulfed Ashley with her signature bear hug.

"Ashley. How's my newest daughter tonight?"

"Great, Mum, and you? Are you going out?"

Darcy kissed her cheek. "I'm glorious and yes, Mrs. Miller and I are going to see a show at Dutch Apple tonight. I think it's called *Oklahoma*. Ever see it?"

"Not yet, but Harry and I have that on our date list."

"I'll let you know if it's good. Have a blessed night." She kissed her son and closed the door behind her.

Ashley turned to her Harry, wrapping herself around him. "We're alone now. Tell me the surprise. I can't wait. Are we going swimming? Mom and I bought a new swimsuit last night." She raised her eyebrows. "Never seen you in swim trunks. Can't wait."

Harry's face turned pink before he gently caressed her lips. His light brown eyes shimmered when he pulled away. "Our dip will be later. Remember that night when I showed you my gladiolas?"

The night they'd started dating. *The night I realized I was in love with you.* "Um-huh."

"I told you I had four passions in life. Remember?"

Her fingers touched his cheek. "Yes."

"But I told you I wasn't ready to show the last one, yet. Tonight, I plan to. Would that be fine?"

We grow closer every day. She remembered it vaguely, however, he'd said *Ashley* was his first and most important passion. "Don't keep me in suspense! Tell me."

"Hey, you two." Ashley turned to find Margaret holding her niece. *Margaret? What's she doing here?*

Margaret addressed her brother. "So you're finally letting her in on our secret, huh?"

Ashley's mind was confused. *Our secret?* Why was his sister holding the baby? "Where's Ellie and Henry?"

Margaret's smile was dazzling. "They had a date with Ben and Sophie. Didn't Harry tell you the three of us are babysitting?"

Ashley's heart fell and she started to tremble inside. Harry would know why. "No, he didn't."

Harry slowly turned her toward him. "My secret involves both of them, but first, come back to my room. I've something to show you."

"Like what?"

His hand was warm where he touched her. "Come see for yourself." He led her down the hall to a door. He opened it and she followed. His room, sparsely decorated, except for dozens of pictures. *All of me.* Her pulse quickened.

"Sit on the bed, princess."

Harry helped her get situated on the mattress and softly kissed her. From his pocket, he pulled a key. "You're only the second person I've ever shared this with." Harry turned and knelt before a large wooden trunk. He unlocked it and raised the lid.

"What's in there?"

Harry lifted several bundles tied in yellow ribbons and sat them next to her.

His face was sober as he searched her eyes. "My life's work." He untied a ribbon and handed her a glossy item.

"A book?"

Harry gently touched the cover. "This was the first. Wrote it for Maggot when she was eight. She was so lonely. A wee girl stuck on a farm with three older brothers. No one to play with. Wanted to do something nice for her."

You wrote these? "These... they're beautiful. Who drew the pictures?"

Harry breathed deeply. "I did."

Ashley inhaled sharply. "No way! These are... can't find the word for it... really cool!" She leafed through the pile of books. "Where'd you get the ideas for all these?"

"It just comes to me. This is who I am, who I really want to be."

Her chest quickly tightened. They were all children's books. For kids she couldn't give him. She quickly wiped her eyes. "I'm sorry, that... I'm just sorry."

"For what?"

"I can't give you what you want most."

Harry knelt and held her hands. "Stop it. I have everything I could ever possibly want, right here in the palm of my hand right now."

"But, they're children's books and..."

"And you and I will share them with the world."

The essence of apple blossoms filled her nose. She turned to see Margaret's smiling face. "We've been waiting for you to come, so you could read the first one out loud to Maggie."

Ashley's heart was in her throat. "But, I-I..."

Harry stood and lifted her up. "We'll choose this book to start. It's called *The Improbable Princess.* About a girl who helps the king find his missing queen. It's Margaret's story, in honor of her helping Henry find Ellie when she was missing."

They walked into the kitchen. Margaret rocked Maggie, holding her so Harry and Ashley could read to her.

Harry held up the book. Maggie stared at the pretty colors while her aunt fed her. Harry's deep voice was so comforting. "Once upon a time when the world was young, there lived a girl with long blonde hair." He stopped and smiled at Ashley. "Your part, princess."

"Okay, um. Her name was Magalena and she was a poor farm girl..."

As the story went on, Ashley was drawn in, not just by the words or pictures, but by the feelings. *Harry's sharing his heart and mind with me.* She saw him on a completely different level, a deeper connection, closer intimacy.

Ashley was sad when the story was over. Harry's face was so handsome, almost beaming. Margaret's reflected the pride for her brother. And little Maggie? She was sound asleep.

"My brother's talented, isn't he?"

Ashley stared at him in awe. "Yes. I-I don't know what to say."

"I do. His books are his closest guarded secret. He told me he was waiting to share them with someone very special. Ashley, I'm glad it's you."

Ashley's heart swelled. *Not as happy as I am.* "Can we read another one?"

Harry's eyes were so full of love. "If that's what you desire, my princess."

They ended up reading an entire series he'd written about a tree squirrel named Charles. Afterwards, they changed into their swimsuits and soaked in Ellie and Henry's hot tub outside. The stars were bright and the moon picturesque, but the item of wonder was the man who sat next to her, arm around her shoulder. Her entire body tingled. *From the warm water jetting around me? Or the man touching my shoulder?*

"So now that you know my deepest secret, what do you think of me?"

Ashley touched the stubble on his cheek. "I never dreamed anyone could make me feel like this. Like a real princess. Like we're one."

Harry's index finger traced her lips. "We are one. Brand this feeling on your heart, because I promise you, every day will be better than the one before. I've waited a lifetime to find you and now that you're here, I'm the happiest person in the world."

The touch of his lips thrilled her deeply inside. *Can life ever be better than this? Heaven had arrived.*

***

Sophie was anxious and tingled all over with anticipation as they waited for the waitress to bring their dessert. Despite the planning she and Benjamin had done as to how they wanted this to go, doubt began to fill her mind. *Only get one shot at this. Suppose we get it wrong?* A glance at Benjamin told her she wasn't the only one worried. Her husband was fidgety. Everything would have to be perfect for this to work out. Their future depended on this one moment in time.

Sophie shifted her eyes across the table to her best friend. Ellie looked happy but tired. Her friend's eyes sparkled as they always did when Henry was around. *She's so lucky to have that man.* Henry stood and offered his hand. Ellie giggled as she took it and pushed her chair back. Sophie shook her head. As she'd seen countless times before, Henry had anticipated his wife's feelings. *How does he do that?* Ellie's voice broke the trance. "Need to powder my nose. Want to join me, Soph?"

Sophie's mouth was dry. It was almost the time in the meal when they had planned to ask. The butterflies in her stomach were giving way to a stampede of wild bulls. "Good idea. I'll keep you company." The women walked to the lavatory.

Ellie's apricot perfume was becoming a tad overwhelming. Her friend studied her in the mirror as she washed her hands. "So when are you going to tell us?"

Sophie avoided eye contact. "Tell you what?" A bitter taste was working its way up her throat.

Ellie's laughter filled the room. "The secret you and Ben have been hiding. Come on, girl! We're besties."

Sophie's chest suddenly tightened dramatically. So difficult to breathe. Her belly rumbled. "Not feeling so well." She made a mad dash for the toilet, barely making it in time. She was retching when she felt Ellie behind her, pulling back her hair.

"It's okay. I'm here." Ellie pulled a large handful of toilet paper and stuffed it in Sophie's hand. A second wave of nausea hit. "Was it something you ate?"

"Don't know. Maybe."

Ellie helped Sophie to stand before enfolding her friend in her arms. Ellie changed her stance to steady her. "You doin' okay?"

The world spun faster. Sophie grabbed the counter, but that didn't help. "So dizzy. Afraid I'm going to pass out."

The door opened and two women walked in. They halted their conversation when they saw Ellie holding Sophie. Ellie barked an order at them. "Her husband's name is Ben Miller. Find him and tell him to get in here, now!"

Before the women could move, the door shook from someone pounding on it. The Scottish voice from the other side was loud. "Ellie, are you all right?"

"No. I need you, Henry."

The door flew open as Henry rushed in. He quickly assessed the situation and swept Sophie in his arms.

His next words were to Ellie. "Are you sick, too?"

"No. Just her." Ellie took Sophie's purse from her hand. "There's a daybed in the corner. Help her there and I'll go get Ben."

Henry placed Sophie on the settee, his hand supporting her head until she was fully reclined. His eyes met hers. She began to calm down. It was Henry's touch. *My best friend, my soulmate.* She reached up and gently touched his face. "Thank you."

"What happened?" Henry grabbed her hand and squeezed it tightly.

"Dinner didn't agree with me, then I got woozy."

"What can I do for you?"

Father my child? Her cheeks heated. "Stay with me 'til Benjy gets here. Please don't leave me. Ever."

His smile told her he understood. "I never will. I promise I'll always be here for you. You believe that, don't you?"

Her vision was blurry. "Yes, I do, with all my heart." The warmth of their friendship filled her soul.

Ben appeared in the door frame. "Sophie! What happened?"

The warmth of her cheeks dissipated. It was her nerves, but she couldn't blurt it out. "The asparagus didn't sit well with me. Mind if we go home now?"

"Of course. Anything you want."

They dropped off the Campbells and Ben drove her home. He helped her inside the door and into the bedroom. Gently, he removed Sophie's shoes and jewelry, then helped her change into bedclothes.

Sophie was deep in thought as Ben held her. Her mind was on Henry.

Ben cleared his throat to get her attention. "It wasn't the asparagus, was it?"

She shook her head. "No. You know me, very well."

His warm lips touched her forehead. "I'm supposed to. I'm your husband, your soulmate, your best friend. It was your nerves, wasn't it?"

"Yes. So afraid we'd blow our one chance."

Ben sighed as his lips brushed her ear. "Quit being so dramatic. Ellie and Henry are our best friends. They'd do anything for us. We just have to get the nerve to ask."

"And the timing has to be just so." Sophie hesitated. "I think I should be the one to ask."

Ben stiffened as he held her. "We talked about this. And agreed. I'll do the asking."

"But Benjy..."

The volume of his voice rose as he spoke. "Sophie, this isn't up for discussion. It took all I had to agree to this. I'll ask, when the time and the mood are right."

She pulled away and faced him. "I don't want to fight. You're right. We did agree." She pulled his face to hers and kissed him. "I love you, Benjy, forever. Please turn out the light."

Ben's smile was the last thing she saw before the room darkened.

Chapter 12

Edmund took a deep breath of the warm night air before walking into the house. *I asked You to help me change. Grant me the courage.* Everyone was waiting for him inside, just as he'd asked. He thought of Tara, and the image of her face filled his mind. *Please don't let this be in vain.* He stepped across the jamb into the love-filled house where his family lived. The aroma of roasted corn was something he usually couldn't get enough of. Tonight it was only a background scent.

The conversations around the dining table ceased as he stood on the threshold of the room. Everyone who really mattered to him was there, except Tara and Margaret. Susan Miller sat next to Ben and Sophie. Henry was holding his daughter while Ellie played with the little girl's feet. Ashley snuggled against Harry on the near side of the table while his mother deposited a large plate of corn on the cob before them. All eyes were on him.

Ellie broke the silence. "There's the man of the hour. We've been discussing this 'major announcement' of yours. Now that you're here, you can break the suspense." Henry's beautiful wife shot him a smile. *She knows.* Sophie would have told her. Or maybe Mrs. Miller did. They were a tightknit clan.

"Bear with me for a moment while I get Maggot on the line." He dialed her number, set his phone to speaker and placed it near his seat. Edmund's hands were soaked with sweat. *Calm down. Can't be so nervous.*

His sister's voice came across the speaker. "Hello, Edmund. Got your text you would call, which was strange because we rarely talk. What's this big announcement you want to share?"

He winced. "I owe you a sincere apology... sorry about treating you like a wretch. You're on speaker and the entire family's here, including Tara's mother and her brother, so watch what you say."

Margaret laughed and said hello. Everyone responded to her.

Edmund felt sweat dripping off his shoulders to the small of his back. He cleared his throat and waited until everyone was looking. "The first part of my announcement is no surprise to anyone. I've not been the best son, brother or friend to anyone here. Truth be told, I've treated you all horridly. I owe a sincere apology."

Henry responded. "That's all right, brother. I know I could have treated you—"

Edmund held up his hand. "Please, let me finish before I lose my courage. Trying to be honorable is foreign to me. I've been a rotten human being thus far. That much we all know. Not only have I treated each of you poorly, I've treated Tara... well, not anything like I should have."

At the mention of Tara's name, Harry's face reddened.

"It's no secret she asked for some time away from me. Time to decide if she still wants to see me or move on." His eyes paused on Susan Miller's face. An older version of her daughter, Mrs. Miller was still quite fetching. She smiled and winked at him. Susan knew what was coming because he'd asked her weeks ago. To his absolute surprise, she'd agreed.

The tip of his nose tingled as he paused to maintain his composure. He rubbed it harshly to drive away the feeling. "Two monumental things will happen on Saturday. Mum has this grand dinner celebration planned in honor of Harry and Ashley's engagement."

His hands were shaking. *Don't look at Ashley.* He engaged Harry's proud eyes instead. "I'm truly happy for you both. But I don't know if I'll make it and I want to explain why."

Darcy's voice contained anger. "He's your brother, for Heaven's sake. What do you mean you—"

"Mum, let me finish, please. Saturday, Tara and I will talk for the first time in a month. I'm going to beg her to forgive me for being a master fool and also to offer her this." From his pocket, he pulled a box containing a solitary diamond set in gold. There was a collective gasp from the women. "I'm asking her if she has it in her heart to marry me." He drew a ragged breath. "Doubt she'll say yes. If she doesn't, it'll crush me. Wouldn't want to ruin your celebration. But if she does, hope beyond measure, say yes, I wouldn't want to take away your joy. I, uh..." He closed his eyes and shook his head. *This sure was a bonny plan.*

Warm arms engulfed him. He didn't have to open his eyes to know who they belonged to. The essence of gladiolas was overwhelming. He opened his eyes, but avoided looking at her. Ashley's laughter lifted his soul as her hug warmed him. "Come on, Edmund. Of course she'll say yes. We'll have a double celebration. We don't mind sharing, do we, Harry?"

Harry pushed back his chair and ambled over. The look on his face said it all. *Not a chance.* Harry would probably thrash him and it wasn't even his suggestion. *I deserve that.*

Harry's demeanor changed as he grabbed Edmund's hand with his. "Princess is right. If Tara says yes, we'll celebrate with you. And she will say yes, guaranteed." Harry grabbed Edmund's head and moved his mouth to Edmund's ear. "Glad to have my brother back." When he moved away, he was smiling.

Edmund was perplexed. Not at all what he'd anticipated. "I, uh, don't know what to say. Do you really think Tara will agree?"

Margaret's voice sounded from the phone. "Of course she will. I'll talk to her, that'll help. Just think, another sister..."

"Maggot, I appreciate the sentiment, but I need to do this by myself."

"Aw, come on. I want to help."

"I know, I know. Probably could use the assistance, but if I can convince her, I want it to be on my own merit. I'm the one who caused this predicament and I'm the one who needs to fix it."

Henry approached him. "I'm proud of you, brother."

"For what? Being a gigantic idiot?"

"No. For being the man I always knew you could be. You've got Pop's blood running through your veins. Blood of excellence and caring, not just of pride. There was no better man than him. He set the example we all should follow. It's your turn to shine."

Everyone took their turn hugging him, as if he was something very special. The encouragement his family gave him was so unexpected. *Don't deserve this.*

The laughter of Sophie and Ellie rolled like a wave as they flowed in from the kitchen. Sophie carried a tray of flutes while Ellie held two bottles of champagne. The women shared a look and started to sing an old Carly Simon song, with their own funny lyrics. "Anticipation. Anticipation, Tara's making him wait, making him wai-ai-ai-ait..." Ellie popped the cork and poured non-stop until all the glasses were filled.

As Sophie passed out the drinks, she shouted into the phone, "Sorry, Maggot. Not in the office or I'd fax you a drink."

Darcy was the one who held her glass the highest. "Lord, bless Edmund's plan and open Tara's heart." Her voice rose a little. "And thank you for bringing my prodigal son home."

***

Tara slipped into the medical provider meeting at the last possible minute. Only one chair was available and that was next to Joseph Rohrer, M.D. She felt her face heat, remembering all Tracy had told her about him and the way he acted when Tara was around. She straightened her skirt before sitting down. Looking up, she caught the conspiratorial look on Tracy's face and also took note of the sly wink from her practice manager.

The well-built, attractive man to her right shot her a whisper. "Fashionably late, as always. Something I like about you. You really look nice this morning, by the way."

Tara turned to give him the stink-eye, but his wholesome smile disarmed her. "Morning to you, too."

Tracy clapped her hands together. "Okay, folks. Got a lot to cover this morning. There's an upgrade coming to the medical record software, new patient codes," she hesitated until the groans died down, "and remodeling plans for the patient waiting room. But first, we have something important to celebrate. Dr. Rohrer, please come here." Tracy smiled at her. "Ms. Miller, can you give me a hand?"

What's she doing? Hopefully she wouldn't embarrass her by revealing anything about their conversation, especially comments Tara had made about how hot Rohrer looked.

Tracy retrieved a box from a table. "Can you get this out, Tara?"

Inside was a beautiful cake sporting a stethoscope decoration. It read 'Happy Birthday, Joe.'

Tara knew her face must be somewhere between candy apple and Maserati red. As instructed, she hoisted the cake. Tracy quickly inserted a candle and lit it.

"Today is Dr. Rohrer's thirtieth birthday. Here, make a wish and blow it out."

Rohrer was all smiles, but instead of looking at the cake, he studied Tara's face. His smile grew in width when he closed his eyes. They opened and he winked at her before blowing out the candle. The staff sang "Happy Birthday" as Tara gave Tracy a hand with cutting and plating the cake. Most of the providers walked up to grab a piece, but Rohrer sat down.

Tracy whispered, almost under her breath to Tara, "Give the birthday boy what he really wants."

Tracy! Tara's heart was in her throat as she carried his cake, and hers, over. He stood until she sat down.

"Thank you, Tara." He hesitated as he studied her. "Any guess what my wish was?"

She swallowed hard. "I don't know. What?"

He lowered his voice. "That you'll have dinner with me tonight."

She started to shake her head, until her heart forced the voice from her. "I'd be honored."

Rohrer's smile was dazzling, even though his lips were blue from the icing. "Just so you know, this is shaping up to be my best birthday, ever."

Tara couldn't believe she'd said yes to his request. When she returned to her office, her eyes gravitated to the picture of Edmund on her desk. She sat in her chair and picked up the frame. What was he doing now? *Do you even miss me?* She couldn't believe he'd actually listened to her about not contacting her. Tara had expected he would have come to see her, but Edmund hadn't followed her wish. While part of her missed Edmund, another part whispered other words. *He's moved on. That's why he hasn't contacted me.*

Tracy's voice startled her. The practice manager stood in front of Tara. "Looks like the two of you made a connection."

Heat flowed to her cheeks. "Don't know what you mean."

"Right. You forget I was there? I could have sworn I heard birds singing, or was it Cupid's cherubs? And what were the two of you whispering about?" Tracy sat across from her and sipped coffee.

Tara considered her friend before walking over to close the door. "He asked me to dinner tonight."

Tracy almost choked on her drink. "What?"

"He asked me out."

"And?"

"And... I said yes."

Tracy touched her fingers to Tara's cheek. "I'm happy for you."

A chill ran down Tara's spine. "It's nothing, really."

"Right. Keep telling yourself that."

Guilt filled her soul. "Edmund and I haven't broken up or anything."

"Really? Is that what your heart says?"

Tara ignored her. "It's just, just a meal with a friend." She turned to face Tracy. "Am I being stupid? I feel like I'm cheating on Edmund."

Tracy's eyes were full of understanding. "It's not a commitment. Just dinner between friends. Isn't that what you just said?"

"Yes, but..."

"Tara. A couple of days ago, you were crying over how that man made you feel. Forgive me for saying this, but I'm afraid he's just been using you. What, three years and no commitment? You don't have to marry Joe or anything else. It's just a meal."

"Suppose I go too far?"

Tracy's face blanched. "You're not considering..."

"No, not that. But what if, what if I give him the wrong impression. Lead him on when I'm not sure about my heart? And tomorrow the time's up when I told Edmund to let me think. Suppose he..."

Tracy reached for her hand. "There's only one thing to do at a time like this. Bow your head."

Tara did as instructed.

"Father, my friend Tara is at a crossroad in her life. Of course You know what's going to happen, but she doesn't. Fill my friend's heart with Your wisdom. Guide her and show her the way. Help her find the happiness she seeks."

***

Edmund carried little Maggie in his arms. Henry and Ellie held hands as they walked into the restaurant in front of him. Harry had his arm around

Ashley's waist. He was glad Ashley was behind him so he wouldn't be tempted to stare at her.

A greeter smiled at them. "How many?"

Ellie answered, "Five and a half."

"Right this way." They were seated at a large booth. Edmund sat next to Harry, away from his temptation, Ashley. A young male waiter appeared and took their drink orders. Edmund noted the way the man openly flirted with Ashley. Harry's fists clenched and Edmund was glad it wasn't him who was getting under his next oldest brother's skin this time.

When the waiter walked away, Henry gave Harry a strange look. "What's the matter with you?"

"Don't like the bloke talking to my fiancée that way. I've half a mind to—"

Ashley's sweet voice rang out. "Come on, you old pot head. He didn't mean anything by it."

Harry growled. "It offends me."

"Stop it. My heart belongs to you. There's nothing to worry about."

The table was silent, but Edmund's curiosity rose. "Why did Ashley call you a pot head? You have a new habit I should know about?"

Harry's words came out between gritted teeth. "No. I would never touch that stuff. Private joke between us, that's all."

Ellie laughed. "Private joke, hmm? I know the truth. Should I tell them, Harry?"

Harry's face was turning red. "Not if you want to remain my favorite sister-in-law."

"I'm your only sister-in-law, but not for long. Right, Edmund?"

Edmund was saved by the return of the waiter. "Here we go." He handed Ashley a Pina Colada she hadn't ordered. "A little something special for the hot young lady, compliments of yours truly."

Harry slapped the drink out of his hand and pushed Edmund off the seat. His voice was loud enough to be heard throughout the restaurant. "I've about had enough of you speaking like that to my girl. And she's not old enough for alcohol." Harry grabbed the waiter's shirt and the drink tray crashed to the floor. "You and me, we're going outside and settle this, now." Harry shoved the waiter toward the front of the restaurant.

Henry leapt up on the table to get around Ellie and Maggie. He jumped down and wrapped his arms around his brother. "Calm down, Harry, right now. He's just a jerk. Take a deep breath and sit back next to Ashley."

Harry wasn't a threat, not the way Henry restrained him. Out of the corner of his eye, Edmund saw the waiter grab the empty tray and raise it over his head. *He's going to hit Harry.* Edmund hurtled in between the waiter and Harry. The edge of the tray smashed down against Edmund's forehead. A galaxy of stars appeared, but Edmund grasped the man's collar and flung him to the floor. He felt his fists clench as he stood over him. "Leave my brother alone or you'll have to deal with me."

A soft hand touched his arm. Ellie's. "Edmund, stop. You're bleeding." She held a napkin against his head. "Let's get you seated."

By now, most of the restaurant staff had arrived and the waiter was hurried away. A woman touched

Edmund's arm. "I'm the manager. Are you all right, sir?"

Henry stood next to him. "Looks like a minor cut. Keep pressure on it and the bleeding will stop." He held his hand up in front of Edmund's face. "How many fingers do you see?"

"Two standing up, two curled and your thumb. I'm fine, I tell you."

The manager spoke again. "Sir, would you like me to call an ambulance?"

"No."

Henry spoke to the woman, "We're leaving."

"What happened?"

Harry piped up. "I'll tell you what happened..."

Ellie interrupted him. "The waiter tried to serve my brother's underage girlfriend a drink she didn't ask for. The boy flirted with her and Harry got angry, rightly so. When my husband restrained Harry, your waiter tried to hit him with the tray. Edmund jumped between them and paid the price."

"I'm sorry, but I think it would be best if you leave."

Ellie gathered Maggie in her arms. "I think so, too."

Edmund was a little dizzy, still seeing stars. Henry linked his arm through Edmund's. "Let's get you to a doctor."

"I told you I'm fine."

A hand touched his shoulder and Edmund turned. Harry, sporting a look Edmund had never seen, studied him. "Edmund. Thank you. Don't know what to say. I never..."

Edmund touched his brother's hand. "That's what brothers do. Mess with one Campbell, you mess with all three."

***

Tara and Joe Rohrer walked into the restaurant. "Thank you for coming, Tara. I've been meaning to ask you out, but I thought you were in a long-term relationship."

She didn't know what to say. She didn't know her status. It would depend on Edmund. "It's your birthday."

Joe's smile was sad. "I see. Thanks for coming along. Hope this place is okay."

I've hurt him. "I like Italian food."

"Me, too."

The greeter approached them. "Two tonight?" Joe nodded. "Booth or table?"

Joe turned toward her. "Have a preference?"

"Booth, please."

After they ordered their drinks and food, Joe was quiet. Tara broke the ice. "So where'd you grow up?"

"Ephrata. My parents had a dairy farm when I was a kid. Lived there most of their life."

"My grandparents had a farm in Paradise. They raised beef cattle. I loved helping them do the farm work."

"They still have the farm?"

"No. They died a couple of years ago and my mom inherited it. She broke the farm into a couple plots. I bought one and built a house there. What about you?"

"My parents sold out just before I graduated from med school. They live in Leola now. Miss the old place."

Tara took a long sip of her drink. "Why'd you get into medicine?"

"It was my fall-back plan."

"Fall-back plan? What was your first choice?"

"To be a fighter pilot. I was accepted at the Naval Academy, but changed my mind. Medicine turned out to be a more interesting field. And you?"

"A childhood friend got cancer. Age six. Almost took her life, but she pulled through. Tough girl. I wanted to help people like her."

"She still alive?"

"Yep. Beat cancer after it came back."

"How's her quality of life?"

Tara studied her glass. *Better than mine. She's engaged.* "Ash's doing very well."

Their meal came and they ate in silence, until Joe put down his utensils. "Can I ask a blunt question?"

She could guess what was coming. "Sure."

"I heard you and your boyfriend were having trouble. Are you two still together?"

"I-I don't really know."

"He's a fool. He should be trying everything he can to keep you. I think you're something else."

They stared at each other. Tara's mouth opened, but nothing came out.

"If you do break up, I would like to date you. Can you make me that promise?"

Before she could answer, she heard a man yelling. "I've had enough..." Her blood chilled. That was Harry Campbell's voice. Tara stood just in time to see the waiter raise a tray over his head, obviously planning on hitting Harry. Edmund rushed in between and took the blow. Fear tore down Tara's spine as she watched the rest of the drama unfold. Her heart went out to Edmund when he stumbled out, supported by Henry.

Joe touched her arm. "Wow. Wonder what that was all about? Things like that just don't happen here."

Tara sat back down, but couldn't concentrate. How badly was Edmund hurt? Her thoughts followed the Campbells as they walked out the door.

Rohrer's face appeared puzzled. "You okay?"

"The violence just bothered me, that's all." She glanced at her watch. "Look at the time. I-I've got to go."

"Something I said?"

"No. I'm pretty tired. Thanks for dinner and Happy Birthday." She gave him a peck on the cheek and hurried out the door.

***

"Here's some ice and Tylenol. This will help." Ellie was being very kind as she took care of him. But then, Ellie had always been nice to him.

"How bad is it?"

"You've got an ugly bruise. The cut's not deep, but it's about two inches long. I'm afraid you'll have a scar."

The scent of peppermint filled his nose. His mum handed him a cup of hot tea. "Drink, boy. I swear, every time I let the three of you out of my sight, you get in trouble. Drink."

Harry's voice was quiet. "That should have been me. Why'd you step in between?"

Ellie squirted something on the cut and pressed a bandage over it. It hurt.

"Because you're my brother. He was going to hit you. I couldn't stand by like a dumb bugger and allow that."

Ellie touched his face. "What can I get you?"

"Nothing. Thanks for everything. Think I'll go outside and sit a spell."

Harry stood. "Keep you company."

They sat on the swing in silence. The clip-clop of a buggy momentarily stopped the chirping of the crickets. As the noise faded, the crickets resumed their serenade.

Harry's voice was soft. "Wanted to say I'm sorry."

"Don't be. I would have acted the same way."

"Wasn't talking about defending Ashley. Sorry you and I were at each other's throats for so long."

"Don't be. It was my fault."

"Takes two to have a fight. Why were you mad at me all these years?"

A shooting star briefly lit the night. "Truth be told, it never was you. I was mad at myself."

"For what?"

"For not being a man. Like you and Henry. Guess that was my way of revolting. God, I was a fool." *Especially for treating Tara like I did.*

"Proved you were a man tonight."

Edmund laughed. "How? By letting that slime hit me?"

Harry's hand rubbed his back. "No. By putting someone else first. You did that without any care for your safety. A sign of a true man is when he stands up for someone else. I don't think I've ever said this, but I'm proud to be your brother."

"Getting in a fight doesn't mean I'm a man. It was childish."

"Wasn't just talking about tonight. Something's come over you. We've all seen it. It's because of what happened with Tara, isn't it?"

Edmund winced, not from his head wound, but because of the pain in his heart. "Yep. Come to realize what a fool I've been. She's got every reason to tell me to take a hike." He turned to face his brother. "I'm scared, Harry. If she leaves me, my world will be over."

Harry shook his head. "If she leaves you, it's her who'll be the fool. Tomorrow's the day. What are you planning to do?"

"To be honest with her, something I've not done well. Tell her how I really feel and beg her to forgive me."

Harry squeezed his hand. "Don't give up. She'll come around. I feel it in my heart. 'Night, brother."

"'Night, Harry."

The screen door swished closed. Edmund stared into the sky. Out here in the country, the stars were so bright, like they were in Scotland. The beauty and depth of the Milky Way stirred something inside. "God, if You're really there, help me. Give me the strength to do this right."

Edmund checked the time on his phone. Just a little before eleven. A calmness came over him. He didn't know the outcome, but it was now in God's hands.

Chapter 13

*T*he ring of her cell phone startled Tara. *Edmund?* It was exactly one minute past midnight. Her thoughts had been on him, concerned over how much pain he was in. She'd had to bite her lip when she walked past the booth where the Campbells had been seated. A bloody napkin was on the table. The phone rang again. She forced herself to calm down. Tara sent a brief prayer for calmness. "Hello?"

Edmund's voice seemed to display relief. "Tara? Thankfully you answered. How've you been?"

"How's your head? Did you get stitches?"

Silence. "How did you know?"

"That's not important. Are you in pain? How are you feeling?"

"Okay, but I really don't want to talk about me. Did I wake you?"

"No. Tell me you're okay, please?"

"I'm fine. I need to ask a favor."

A favor? He calls for a favor? "What is it?"

"I don't want to keep you up, but I wanted to ask you something. May I?"

Her whole body trembled. She realized how much she'd missed the sound of his voice. "Yes, yes, of course. Would you rather come over and ask it in person?"

"I'd love that, however, I want to do this formally. Is that all right?"

What did he mean, 'wanting to do it formally'? The saliva in her throat curdled. *He's going to break up with me.* "I guess. What did you want to ask me?"

"I wanted to ask if I could pick you up at four fifteen this morning. We need to talk and I have somewhere very important to take you. I know the hour will be early, but this is time sensitive. Would you be amenable to that?"

"Four fifteen is the middle of the night! What could be time sensitive at that hour of the day?"

The sound of his laughter woke the butterflies in her stomach. "That's the surprise. Would you be ever so kind as to allow me the company of your presence then?"

After four weeks, how could his words make her weak in the knees? She hesitated. Only four hours from now. She'd never be able to get back to sleep. Not without knowing what this was all about. "Is this something we can do now or later in the day? A girl needs her beauty sleep, you know."

His voice was soft. "Lesser women might, but not you. Will you allow me the preciousness of your company?"

She was confused. It had been four weeks, four very long weeks, but his words and tone touched her deeply. *Are we breaking up or making up?* She nodded, before realizing he couldn't see her nod. "I-

I guess that would be okay. Do I need to dress up any special way?"

"Tara, it is not about what you wear, but about who you are. That being said, you might wish to put on a dress, actually your prettiest dress. It might be important later."

A dress? At four in the morning? "Important later? Edmund, talk to me. What's going on?"

He laughed again. "It's a surprise, but I think you might be delighted. I'm going to hang up now, so sweet dreams. Until I see you in person, you'll walk the fields of my dreams. Good night, Tara."

With that exchange, he disconnected. Tara stared at her phone in disbelief. Where in the world could they be going at four in the morning? She knew sleep was not on the menu, so she got out of bed and headed for the shower. In amazement, she started to get ready.

**

After Edmund hung up, he studied his face in the mirror. She hadn't told him off. Was there still hope? *Please, God...* He understood it all so clearly, now. Tara *was* the girl of his dreams, the love of his life. Edmund had to find some way to get her to forgive him or he would kick himself in the rear forever. He walked to his room to get everything ready.

Edmund reached for the bag hanging behind his bedroom door. He wanted everything to be perfect for her. A box fell out of the bag. He opened the lid, allowing the illuminance of the overhead LED lamp to showcase the beauty of the diamond. Entranced,

Edmund studied it, but the only thing he really saw was the twinkle of Tara's eyes in his mind.

***

The second hand on the clock seemed to be in slow motion as Tara waited. She took her time, dressing in her favorite dress after applying makeup. She studied her face in the mirror, not really happy with what she saw. Time had been her enemy. Her hair looked flat. The crow's feet around her eyes were prominent. Tara didn't know if it was because she was tired or because of her age. The last four weeks without Edmund had been unimaginably miserable. But as Tara replayed their conversation, she was amazed he'd spoken with her like he always did. As if they'd seen each other last night.

At three thirty, she could stand it no more. She sauntered outside, basking in the warm night air. Her heart continued to beat as if nothing was different. But it was. Everything would change in a few minutes. *What will my life be like after this?*

A rooster crowing from inside Ben and Sophie's barn momentarily drew her attention.

What was going to happen? Her mind was in fast gear. Some of the anxiousness was because of her curiosity, but more of it was because she realized how much she'd missed Edmund. At four ten, the lights of his car lit up the front of Ellie's home in the distance. She was standing in the drive when he pulled up.

Her mouth fell open when Edmund stepped out of the car. To her utter amazement, he was dressed in a tuxedo. The only other time she'd seen him dressed in a tux was when Ellie married Henry. *What's going on?*

Edmund walked toward her, taking her hand without a word before opening the door. His hand trembled at her touch. Tara slid in the seat and reached up to hold him. She couldn't wait any longer. Edmund needed to kiss her, to prove this wasn't a dream. Edmund pulled away and quickly gave her a peck on her forehead. "Not quite yet, Tara, not quite yet."

She shook her head in confusion as he climbed into the driver's seat. "Edmund, what's going on? I missed you so much. Don't you even want to kiss me?"

His smile was illuminated by the dash lights. "Please bear with me. I prefer to drive us there in silence, but I'd love to hold your hand. May I?"

Despite her confusion, Tara simply nodded. *This* was *going to be a happy ending, wasn't it? Please?* To go to all this effort to break up would be unimaginably cruel. They drove in silence along the main road, heading west. Her heart raced as she watched his expression, backlit as the lights from passing cars flickered through the windshield. His smile was the most beautiful sight she'd ever seen, especially when he glanced her way.

***

Four weeks ago, he'd thought differently of this wonderful girl sitting next to him. His heart now threatened to beat out of his chest. Back then, he hadn't even been sure he loved her. But the time away had changed everything. After their distance, he realized not only did he love her, he needed Tara. Edmund wanted to spend his entire life with her. She really was the one. Tara hadn't changed one iota in the last month, but he had. Inside, he was a much different man. A man he was proud to be.

As the miles rolled by, his mind drifted back on their time apart. Twenty-eight days of pure hell. It hadn't taken very long for his eyes to be opened, to understand what he really was. A very devious and nasty piece of humanity, if he was even that. Worse than that. A colossal fool was what he'd been. Within the first week, his heart told him what he needed to do. He'd bought Tara an engagement ring. *Would she accept?* He'd find out within the hour.

***

They crossed the mighty Susquehanna, leaving the interstate at the first exit after the bridge. Edmund pointed the car up the hill as they drove through Wrightsville. *Where are we going?* Tara tried to piece together the destination. *Sam Lewis State Park?* He'd taken her there in the past, but never in the dark. That couldn't be it, unless they were going to watch the sun rise. That might be it.

The scent of his aftershave filled the car. *He's wearing a tux.* Why was he so dressed up? And what was the reason he'd asked her to don her best dress? A wonderful thought crossed her mind. *Wait, could it be?* No, that was just a cruel vision. Tara quickly rejected the thought. It was doubtful Edmund really loved her, truly, inside his heart. Maybe this was his way of letting her down gently.

Just before the crest, he turned onto a county road. *It* is *Sam Lewis*. Edmund parked the car in the empty lot. He retrieved something from the back seat before opening her door. Even in the dim pre-dawn light, she could see his smile.

His hand was warm when he offered it to her. Warm, but shaky. "Are we watching the sunrise?"

"Patience, my dear Tara."

In silence, they walked to a bench at the highest point. Off to the east, the sky was waking, turning orange. He turned to smile at her and she noticed the large bandage on his forehead. "Your head, where he hit you. Does it hurt?"

"It's fine. Keep your eyes to the east. Something spectacular's about to happen."

Something spectacular? He knew how she loved astronomy. Tara wracked her mind, trying to remember if there was a comet or meteor shower. Nothing. Edmund stood and her attention was drawn to him. How had she missed him carrying a basket? His back was turned as he rummaged through the container. He seemed to be struggling with something. A loud pop disturbed the early morning silence. A gurgling noise. Liquid being poured? *Champagne? Oh my God!*

The morning light was increasing. The distant horizon was trimmed in hues of amber and ginger. Edmund walked between her and the sunrise. He held two wine glasses. Her hand hesitated before taking the one he offered.

He closed his eyes briefly before breaking the silence. "Tara, these last four weeks have been both a bane and a blessing. I missed you so much and regret the squandered opportunity to be together. Yet this time apart made me assess myself. When I analyzed my life, I realized I was..." He stopped and drew a deep breath. "I'm ashamed of myself, of the fool I'd become. I was rude to many people but what I regret most is how I treated you. You gave me nothing but love and I took that for granted."

Edmund glanced over his shoulder. Rays of sunshine were breaking over the distant hills.

He shifted his weight and continued. "I doubt you'll believe me, but I've changed, Tara, really changed. I was so stupid and I beg you to forgive me."

The rising sun set the crown of his head aglow. "I want you to know I love you, Tara. With all my heart." Much to her surprise, Edmund dropped to one knee, setting his glass aside before fumbling with something in his pocket.

Tara suddenly realized what was about to happen. *Is this real?* She pinched herself to make sure. *Never in a million years...* The words spilled out before she had a chance to think. "I love you, too."

He kissed her hand. "In that time apart, I discovered what I want my destiny to be. I want to share my life with you, as my wife." He opened a white jeweler's box. An errant ray of sunlight set the gem on fire. Her eyes were drawn to the dazzling diamond in the ring. "I'm going to ask you something precious in just a second, but before I do, I want to beg your forgiveness for taking you for granted. My eyes have been opened. Is there any way you can possibly forgive me for being a fool?"

Her emotions were running away. She fanned her face to cool herself. Their time together flashed before her, yet she could only utter one word. "Yes."

Edmund closed his eyes and drew another deep breath before continuing. "Tara, I love you, I need you, I want you. Not just for a day, but every second of the rest of my life. Tara Suzanne Miller, would you do me the undying pleasure of joining your life with mine, as my wife?"

Her breath was coming in clumps. "Are you serious? This isn't just some cruel joke, is it?"

He set the ring on the ground and touched her cheeks. As he breathed, he bit his lips together. "After the way I've treated you, I can understand your confusion. No, this is no joke. I want to marry you."

Any second now I'll wake up. She was silent.

His hands fell away. "If the answer is no, I understand."

Tara's voice still wouldn't come. Her chin trembled.

Edmund looked away, but the emotion staining his cheek moved her. "It was... I'm sorry, truly sorry." He buried his head in his hands.

Tara's vision was blurry as she threw her arms around him and whispered in his ear, "Yes. Yes. I've wanted to marry you since the night we met."

He pushed her away to arm's length, eyes opened wide. "Did I hear you right? You'll m-marry me? After all I've done?"

Her lips met his as she nodded. "Um-huh."

Edmund's breath was ragged. "Yes?"

"Yes. I love you. Time will never change that."

He held her hand. "May I place the ring on your finger?"

Every nerve in her body tingled. "Please."

He slipped it on. The ring fit perfectly. Edmund pressed his lips to her fingertips.

"It's like it was made for me."

"It is, just for you. Your mother loaned me one of your rings for sizing."

"Mom did what?" Tara stood and reached for him.

He didn't move from his knee. "Please sit down. There's more."

More? "What else could there be?" Tara sat on the edge of the bench and watched as he removed a second jewelry box from his other pocket.

"The reason we're dressed up is for this." He opened the box to display the exact set of wedding rings she's dreamed about all her life.

Tara's hands covered her mouth. "These rings... how could you know?"

"You pointed them out to Sophie and Ellie once upon a time. They both came along to make sure I chose the right ones."

Her breath was rapid. "What's all this mean?" His look made her hands tremble.

"I wore this tuxedo and asked you to wear your finest dress, in case you wanted to get married today. If you want to wait and wed in a ceremony later, that's fine, too." Edmund wrapped his arms around her. "I've changed, Tara, really changed. I want exactly what you desire. Marriage, children, happily ever after. I wanted us to be prepared for what you wanted. I love you today and forevermore."

Tara's head was spinning, like it did when she'd had too much to drink. But her champagne hadn't been touched. Holding his hand became difficult because hers were trembling so badly.

Her voice was shaky. "What do you want? Do you want to get married today?"

He kissed her cheek. "Only if you desire. You're my dream and I'll wait forever, if that's what you crave."

Her arms wrapped around his neck. "This is what I crave most in life." Their lips blended together as the sunlight fully ensconced them.

Chapter 14

llie sipped the champagne as her husband Henry toasted Harry and Ashley. Maggie May was asleep in the swing under the watchful eye of Grandma Darcy. "Ashley, hopefully you won't come to your senses before my brother is lucky enough to marry you." Laughter rippled through the barn as Harry turned another shade of red. "Seriously, we're thrilled to have you join our family. Harry's never been happier and everyone knows why. Because of you, the young lady he's in love with."

Henry glanced at Ellie and she could feel his love pouring to her. *So strong and warm.* She blew a kiss his way.

Henry cleared his throat. "The wish Ellie and I have for you is that your love will grow as deep as ours in time."

Ashley ran over and embraced Henry. Harry also hugged his eldest brother after Ashley released him. The engaged couple looked so happy.

A hand touched Ellie's shoulder. It was Margaret. Her sister-in-law smiled, but Ellie felt the despair coming from her. "You hear from Edmund?"

Ellie sadly shook her head. "No. I must have texted him like thirty times. I tried calling, too, but no answer."

Margaret nodded her head. "Tara dumped him. I can see why, in a way. Then again, at times they seemed so happy. You think that's why he didn't show?"

Ellie frowned. "I imagine it would be hard. Seeing Harry and Ashley so happy. Knowing that's not in the cards right now for him."

"I guess. You think Edmund likes Ash?"

What an odd question. Ellie studied the fair-headed girl next to her. There was something about Margaret and the way she could read people. "Why do you ask?"

"Nothing, I guess. Just seems he avoids her. Never seen him talk to her."

Hmm. Now that you mention it. "I never picked up on that, but maybe you're right. But I don't see how anyone couldn't like Ashley."

A smile graced Margaret's lips. "I agree. Such a wonderful girl. So kind, so sweet. And the way she glows when she's around Harry. I'm so happy he found her. Glad to have her as my sister. A special girl. Maybe not as special as you, but in time..."

Ellie knew her dimples appeared. "Um-huh. I love happy endings."

A voice came over the speakers. The DJ. "This next song is dedicated to Ashley and Harry. *Keeper of the Stars,* by Tracy Bird." All talking stopped as Harry escorted Ashley to the center of the celebration barn. As the music played, Harry danced with his Ashley. Even from a distance, Ellie could see the stars in their eyes.

A sudden flash of light caught her attention. Sunlight streamed in through the exterior door. *Edmund.* He entered, head down. Both Ellie and Margaret worked their way to him.

Margaret reached him first and hugged her brother. "Edmund. So good to see you." The look on his face wasn't good. "Are you alone?"

He didn't meet their eyes. "Appears that way, doesn't it?"

Ellie wrapped her arms around him. "I'm so sorry. Why don't you come over and sit next to me? We'll talk."

Margaret swept his hair from his eyes. "I know it hurts. I'll sit with you, too."

He shook his head. "No need for that. Today's supposed to be a time of happiness and celebration, isn't it?"

Ellie nodded.

Suddenly, Edmund's face lit up. "Then let's celebrate!" He pushed open the door and Tara ran in, wrapping Edmund in her arms.

Margaret's mouth dropped open. "Tara? What's this mean?"

The music stopped and Ellie turned to see the entire crowd staring at the four of them. Harry pulled Ashley with him as they ran over.

Harry's gaze alternated between Tara and Edmund. "Well?"

Tara stuck her arm out in front of her, wrist bent down and fingers splayed to show off the ring. "Ta-da!"

Edmund's voice was clear as he shouted out loud, "She said yes! Tara and I are engaged!"

Pandemonium broke out. Harry lifted Edmund in a bear hug and spun him around. "I told you she'd agree."

Ellie, Ashley and Margaret all grabbed Tara in a group hug. Out of nowhere, Sophie appeared, leaping onto the four girls. Her momentum knocked the women to the floor. Sophie was crying as she shouted, "The five of us are real sisters now."

Henry appeared and shook his youngest brother's hand. "Congratulations. I'm happy for you. And so, so proud."

Edmund pounded his brother's back. "Thank you for setting the example."

Darcy and Susan Miller were suddenly there, Jessica Snyder in tow as she held little Maggie. Both mothers took their turns hugging Edmund. It was a good fifteen minutes before the hugs began to wind down.

Ellie's heart was full of happiness, for Harry and Edmund. *So blessed to have this family*. Ashley approached Edmund, arms wide open. The average person wouldn't have noted, but Ellie did. Edmund's face turned white. Ashley embraced him. Edmund's body was stiff.

"Edmund, so happy for you. I can barely contain myself." She moved her lips toward his, but Edmund turned his head, allowing her to graze his cheek. He barely touched her shoulder before pulling away.

"Thank you, Ashley. I'm happy for both you and Harry." He untangled himself and walked over to hold Tara's hand.

Ellie caught the look of disappointment in Ashley's eyes. Ashley shrugged, then smiled when Harry pulled her in for a quick kiss. Ellie glanced at Margaret, who had also been watching.

Maggie started to cry. Ellie took the baby from Jessica and sniffed her behind. She shot a smile at Henry. "Someone needs her diaper changed. I'll take her over to the house. She's probably hungry, too."

Henry laughed. "Changing her bottom is my job. I'll come along."

Margaret touched Henry's arm. "You're the master of ceremonies. I'll go with Ellie. Stay here. We'll be back in a jiffy."

That's strange. Margaret followed Ellie as they walked toward her home. Margaret was silent, but her face looked troubled. Once inside, Margaret changed her namesake, then passed the little one to mommy for feeding time.

Ellie was curious. After Maggie was settled at her breast, she sought out Margaret's eyes. "What's going on?"

Margaret's hands were trembling. "You were there. Did you see Edmund's reaction when Ashley hugged him?"

"Yeah. I think you're right. He doesn't seem to like her. Wonder why?"

Margaret pulled her hair into a ponytail. "You're wrong."

"About what?"

"Edmund. Not liking her. It's worse than I thought. It's not that he doesn't like Ashley."

Ellie's eyes widened. "Then what is it?"

"I know my brother. It's plain as the nose on my face."

"I don't understand."

Margaret's eyes were intense. "I'm afraid he's in love with Ashley."

***

Sophie could barely wait for Ben to close their door. Excitement tingled through her entire body. She leapt into Ben's arms. "Oh Benjy, what a glorious day."

His lips found hers. Sophie kissed him so intensely her lips hurt. "Benjy, did you feel it?"

His laughter was like summer rain. "Feel what, your kiss? You haven't kissed me like that since our wedding night. Are you in a special mood?"

Her cheeks heated. "No, not that. Not right now. Did you feel it?"

He studied her with curiosity obvious in his eyes. "Sometimes I just can't read your mind. Enlighten me."

Sophie drew a deep breath. "There's so much happiness all around us. I think the time's just right."

Ben's eyes widened. "You mean... to ask them?"

Sophie was jumping up and down. "Yes! Don't you feel the same way?"

Ben was amused. The look on his face was like it always was when he thought she had a crazy idea. A smile slowly covered his face. "I think you're right. How should we do it? Go out or invite them over?"

Her breathing slowed down. Part of her expected him to reject her idea. "We should go out.

No, we should do it privately. Invite them over. Tonight."

Ben's hands were shaking as he touched her face. "I love you."

They spent the next twenty minutes discussing how to get it just right. Sophie was filled with anticipation as Ben pulled out his cell. He put it on speaker.

"Hello?"

"Hey, Henry. Quite a day, wasn't it?"

"Ben. Yes, it was. Were you as shocked as I was that Tara said yes?"

"Kind of. Actually, it was a total surprise. I hope they'll be as happy as our marriages turned out to be." He winked and smiled at Sophie.

Ask him!

"So what's up?"

"Uh, Sophie and I were thinking that maybe you and Ellie would like to join us for dinner."

Sophie whispered to him. "Tell them not to bring Maggie."

"Yes, just adults tonight. Can you get a sitter?"

There was hesitation. "Maybe not tonight. Haven't had much time with my daughter today."

Sophie could read Ben's reaction without him expressing it. "I see."

"Maybe tomorrow?"

Sophie nodded her head so violently she developed a muscle spasm.

"Sounds great." He raised his eyebrows as he looked at Sophie. "Say about six?"

"Let me check with Ellie." Henry's voice could be heard relaying the information to his wife. He came back on quickly. "Works for us. What should we bring?"

Sophie blurted out her answer. "Nothing, just yourselves."

Henry laughed. "Sophie. How is my dear friend?"

"Just glorious and bubbly."

"Okay. See you then. 'Night."

Ben had just disconnected when Sophie launched herself into his arms. "We're going to have a baby."

***

Ellie placed her sleeping daughter in the bassinet. She reached down and kissed her baby girl. Henry walked in, closed the door and stripped off his shirt. Ellie felt his exhaustion. She kissed him gently.

Henry smiled. "I love you, too."

He looked so handsome. Henry rubbed his arm. He had pain again, like he did anytime the weather changed. Her eyes went to the massive scar that covered the skin on his left arm just above the elbow. Where he'd taken the bullets the night he rescued her.

"It hurts tonight, doesn't it?"

His lips curled into a tired smile. "I'd ask how you know, but that would be silly. Good chance it will rain tomorrow."

His feelings of love were coming in loud and clear. She softly touched the side of his stomach, to the left and just above the navel. The place where she'd stabbed him. The memory of that moment filled her. He winced momentarily before taking her in his arms. *Almost lost you that night.*

Henry kissed her lips, his taste lingering on her tongue. "You didn't know it was me. And you'll never lose me. We'll be together, forever."

Her fingertips traced his cheeks. "You're my hero."

Inquisitiveness filled his eyes. "Something's on your mind. What is it?"

"How do you do this?"

"Do what? Read your mind?"

A giggle escaped her lips. "Yes."

Henry rubbed his nose against her. "That's simple. We're one, inside. Now tell me. What are you thinking of?"

Ellie sat next to him on the bed, holding his hand. "An observation your sister made today."

With his fingers, he turned Ellie's head toward him to gaze into her eyes. "Maggot? What observation?"

"About Edmund. Do you think he likes Ashley?"

"I dunno. I think his mind has been weighing heavily on Tara recently. Why do you ask?"

She kissed his fingertips. "Today when Ashley hugged him, he was like a board, all stiff and stuff."

Henry's eyebrows curved as he considered what she'd said. "That's not like Edmund at all. Is that what made Maggot think he doesn't like her?"

"No. She got something different out of it. It's been nagging at me all day."

"What did my sister say?"

"She thinks Edmund is in love with Ashley."

Henry's eyes widened. "What?"

"Yeah, that's what I thought, too. Then I got to thinking, every time I've seen the two of them anywhere close, he avoids her like the plague. And that's not like Edmund."

He nodded. "I agree. The boy's way too touchy with women. How'd he treat you today?" She read his mind and the thought made her laugh.

"Like a gentleman. He doesn't dare grope me, not since you took him outside at our rehearsal dinner."

His reaction wasn't what she expected. He sat up straighter on the bed. "He deserved more than I gave him. But Ashley, this is very odd, indeed."

"Do you think he's in love with her?"

"It took him almost three years to realize he was in love with Tara. He's only known Ashley a few weeks. Infatuation maybe, but no, not love."

Ellie bit her lip. "Just watch the way he reacts to her. I'm concerned what would happen if Harry found out."

Henry shook his head. "He'd beat Edmund within an inch of his life. Did I tell you I had a long talk with Harry about his anger issues?"

"That's good. Ash confided his temper really scares her. She's afraid to mention it because he might get upset with her."

Maggie babbled in her sleep. Henry walked over to check on his daughter. "I hope in time Harry and Ashley will grow close enough to talk about everything. Like..."

Ellie finished his sentence. "Like we do." Ellie framed Henry's cheeks and kissed his lips. "What we have is so special, so perfect. I love you so much."

"I know. And I love you exactly the same amount as you love me. You're my world, Ellie. My brothers will have to figure it out on their own." Henry's lips found the side of Ellie's neck. "As for me and my wife, we'll live forever in paradise."

Chapter 15

Ellie pushed her empty plate back toward the center of the table. "Sophie, you make the best lasagna."

"Oh, it's nothing. One of the few things I learned from my mother." Sophie turned to search Ben's eyes.

Wonder if they'll tell us tonight. Ellie squeezed Henry's hand while smiling at the couple across the table. "Inviting us over for dinner was a great suggestion. I can't tell you how much I needed a little time away from the baby. She takes so much out of me."

The room suddenly lit up from a lightning flash. Henry laughed at his bride and then kissed her hand. With merriment in his eyes, he quipped to the Millers. "Ellie makes it sound like she's the one doing all the work, all the time. She neglects to tell you she hasn't yet had the need to change a single diaper. Don't sit too close to her. That last flash was a warning. God might just strike her down for fibbing." He turned to kiss her nose. "I do believe we have been sharing responsibilities quite fairly."

Ellie playfully smacked his leg. "If you had someone waking you at all hours of the night because they were hungry, you'd be tired, too."

Henry gazed at her without a word.

Ellie suddenly grasped him and kissed him.

Sophie smiled as she interrupted. "Hi. Don't know if you've noticed, but the two of us are also in the room."

If her face was as red as Henry's, it was quite embarrassing. Henry's voice was low as he responded, "Sorry. Haven't had much time together... alone time, I mean."

Sophie propped her head in her hands and smiled at them. "You two. Sometimes I wonder if you're trying to compete with us." Her smile disappeared. "You two are so lucky. You have everything. Love, happiness and a beautiful daughter. I'm so envious."

Ellie knew her friend well enough to know when she wanted to talk. Now was one of those times. She reached across the table to hold Sophie's hand. "Tell us how it's going."

That was all the encouragement Sophie needed. The floodgates opened. Over the next half hour, Sophie filled both of them in on everything. Ellie noted Ben also contributed, quite a bit. *How odd. Sophie was usually the spokesperson.* The pair laid it all out on the table, from Ben's sterility to adoption considerations and insemination options.

Ben uncorked a bottle of wine and filled their glasses. "Sophie and I've come to an agreement." His hand was shaking as he held his glass. "We don't want to adopt. Sophie will carry our child. Join me in celebration."

Sophie reached over to grasp Ellie's hand. She whispered, "We're going to need your help with this, from both of you."

Ellie could feel what was in Henry's heart, compassion for their closest friends. Henry reached across the table to hold both their friend's hands. "You know we'll do whatever we can to help you. You can count on us, even when the rest of the world is against you. You're our closest friends and I owe you. The only ones who believed in me when Ellie was missing."

The room grew quiet. Ellie thought it was strange that Sophie wasn't looking at them.

Henry's voice startled her. "So when will the happy event occur?"

Sophie and Ben's eyes met. Some private, unspoken conversation was happening between them. Sophie nodded and Ben closed his eyes briefly before turning to face Henry. "It depends."

Henry's curiosity filled Ellie. "Depends on what, Ben?"

Ben's face turned bright red. Sophie drew close to her husband. Ben cleared his throat. "It depends on you, Henry."

Henry turned to Ellie and they shared a questioning look. He turned back toward Ben. "Why does it depend on me?"

Ben's face was sober. "We want you to father our child."

The emotions flooding from Henry were confusing. Shock. Happiness for them. Caring. Yet something else.

Sophie's fingers were trembling as she touched Ellie's hand. "If it's all right with you."

Ellie could feel Henry's anxiety. She patted his hand before standing and walking around the table toward her friend. Sophie met her halfway there, arms engulfing her. "Of course. Henry and I would be honored for him to father your child."

A sudden noise caught Ellie's attention. She swiftly turned to see Henry picking up his chair. He must have knocked it over. The look on his face chilled Ellie. Henry quickly walked out the door and closed it loudly behind him without another word.

***

The scent of baby's breath and jasmine engulfed her as she entered the door. Tara felt happier than she'd ever dreamed possible. Her mother, Susan, accompanied her in the quest for the perfect dress. Tara had driven past this boutique hundreds of times, always dreaming of someday picking out her own wedding gown. *And today, my dreams are coming true.*

They were right on schedule for the appointment. A red-haired lady extended her hand as she smiled. "So, you're Tara?" Tara nodded. "I'm Emma, your bridal consultant. So nice to meet you in person. I have the dresses you selected ready. Follow me, you lucky bride to be."

Tara's top five picks were on hangers in the dressing room. Emma assisted her in putting them on. Susan waited on a cushioned sofa, excited to watch her daughter model them. The first two were nice, but not exactly what Tara wanted. However, the third was exquisite. The strapless gown was a bead and lace-covered satin dress, snowy white. The beads formed a heart in the center of her chest. Tara loved the way it accentuated her figure.

Susan covered her mouth when Tara strolled out. "Oh Tara, it's beautiful." Susan walked around Tara, taking it in. She held her daughter's hand. "I think this is the best one yet. Look at your eyes. This, it's the one you want, isn't it?"

Yes, yes. "Do you think Edmund will like it?"

Before her mother could answer, a deep voice responded. A man's words. "He'd be a fool not to think you're the most beautiful woman, ever. And I'm not talking about the dress."

Tara turned to see Joe Rohrer standing there. She opened her mouth, but nothing came out. Her mother retreated to the couch. Tara finally found her composure while Joe stood there. "This is a surprise. What are you doing here?"

Joe's smile seemed to hide disappointment. "My sister is trying on gowns today. Her fiancé is deployed along the DMZ in Korea right now. They're getting married as soon as he musters out."

Tara's hands were sweaty. "D-do you like my dress?"

His eyes drank her in, making her knees shaky. Joe looked away, softly speaking while not engaging her eyes. "I've never seen a more beautiful sight. Guess you two got everything straightened out, eh?"

"Y-yes, we did. Edmund proposed to me. We're planning a June wedding."

He hesitated and she couldn't read the look on his face. *Is he holding something back?* "He's a very lucky man. Luckiest man alive, if you ask me."

Was he trying to say more? "Thank you."

"I, uh, well. Congratulations. To both of you."

Tara searched her mind for the right thing to say. *Why is my heart pounding so hard in my chest?*

Another woman's voice called out, "Joey, how's this one look?"

Rohrer turned his attention to a very petite woman with curly brown hair standing in front of another dressing room. "Be there in a second." He looked back at Tara. Hurt was obvious in his eyes. "Nice seeing you again. Best wishes, Tara."

She could barely get the words out. "Thanks. See you at the office. Bye."

"Yeah. See ya." Rohrer turned and reached for his sister's hand. "Franny, don't you make that dress look beautiful?"

A chill ran down Tara's back. *What just happened?* Her heart began to ache.

***

Jessica Snyder tried to put aside the memories that flooded her mind. How many times had she sat here in this exact chair, waiting for the doctor to come out and reveal the findings? The touch of warmth against her hand startled her. Harry.

"It will be fine."

Jessica fought to control the emotions. "It hasn't always been."

"Maybe, but something's different this time."

She turned to search his eyes. "What's that?"

"You don't have to be the strong one anymore. I'm here, now. You've a son to lean on when things are tough." Harry reached for her and comforted her in his strong arms.

"Mrs. Snyder?" A nurse stood before her. "Dr. Longstreet wants you to come back now." The nurse smiled at Harry. "Ashley asked for you to come back, too, Mr. Campbell."

Harry held her hand tightly as they walked back the hall. *Please Lord, good news.* Jessica's heart was in her throat. They entered the room. Ashley was dressed in the pink skirt and western shirt Harry had given her. Her daughter's feet dangled from the examining table. Jessica's vision blurred as she remembered Ashley sitting there long ago, feet dangling just like when she'd been diagnosed with cancer at age six.

Dr. Longstreet extended his hand, smiling at her. "Good to see you again, Mrs. Snyder. Please have a seat."

Ashley reached for Jessica's hand. Harry still clung to the other one.

"I've got very good news. The results of all tests were negative for any sign of cancer."

Jessica doubled over, wetness moistening her cheeks. Harry knelt next to her, arm around her. "Thank God."

"It's too soon to be one hundred percent sure, but I believe her cancer is in remission. Still, I'd like to see her back in six months for a checkup. Okay?"

Jessica could only nod her head. Ashley was beside her, wrapping her tiny arms around her mother. Ashley whispered so only Jessica could hear. "We did it, Mom. Thanks to you."

Dr. Longstreet said goodbye, allowing Jessica time to regain her self-control. Her voice was still shaky when it came out. "I think a celebration is in order. Let's go to Iron Hill Brewery. My treat."

Ashley lifted her chin. "We'd love that, but there's something important Harry and I need to do first, and we want you to come with us."

"What?"

Ashley's smile was mischievous. "You'll see."

Her daughter knew her way around Hershey Medical Center. She led the trio to the children's cancer ward. Ashley walked up to the nurse's station. "Hi, ladies."

Three of the nurses let out squeals of laughter as they charged around the desk to greet not only Ashley, but also Jessica. And Jessica remembered them well. They'd been there for her during the dark days, comforting her when it looked like Ashley might not survive. Jessica held on tightly to her favorite nurse, Tammy.

Ashley's strong voice commanded their attention. "Did you do what I asked?"

Tammy was all smiles. "Yep. Everyone's waiting for you."

Confusion. *Waiting for Ashley?*

Tammy ushered them into a common area. A half dozen or so children filled the room, some in wheelchairs, two in their mother's arms, and one in a bed with tubes in her little arms. Parents were gathered with them. Tammy cleared her throat. "Hi, everybody. I want to introduce Ashley Snyder, soon to be Ashley Campbell. This young lady is special. She fought cancer and won, not once, but twice. She's living proof that miracles do happen." Tammy palmed her eyes and hugged Ashley again.

Jessica was astounded at the sight. Not that long ago, Ashley had been the one fighting for her life, and now?

Ashley was smiling ear to ear. "You're fortunate to be here, in this wonderful place. Surrounded by the best doctors and nurses in the world. This is a place of love and hope." Jessica watched as an errant drop of moisture trickled from her daughter's eye. Ashley sniffled, wiped it away and focused on a light fixture momentarily.

Harry walked over, his hand gently grasping Ashley's. Harry slipped a backpack from his shoulder. *Did he have that the whole time?*

"My life was saved and forever changed by the people who touched me here. So much that I want to give you a gift. My purpose in life is clear now. I want to pay back the kindness I was given." Her daughter lifted Harry's hand to her lips. "Our mission in life is to spread love. My fiancé writes children's books and we're going to read a couple of them to you today."

Jessica's mouth dropped open. *Harry writes kid's books?*

"The first one is a story about a little girl who had cancer." Ashley sent a sly smile at Harry, who immediately blushed. "He won't admit it, but he wrote it about me." Her daughter pulled a shiny pink book from the backpack. "This one is called, 'Prayers

Do Get Answered'." She opened the book, displaying a beautiful illustration of a young, blonde-haired girl in a hospital bed with a thermometer in her mouth. "It was a dark, cold rainy day when Angela's parents took her to the hospital. Angie had been sick for a long time..."

When Ashley finished the book, there wasn't a dry eye between all the adults. She read three more to the children. Then Harry and Ashley talked with each family, giving each a signed children's book and praying with them.

Jessica was quiet, yet filled with warmth and wonder during the drive to the restaurant. Finally seated, they had just given their orders. She watched as Ashley smiled at her, snuggling against Harry.

"So what'd you think, Mom?"

Amazement. Shock. Love. "I don't know what to say, other than I'm so proud of you." She turned to Harry. "And you? Utterly unbelievable."

Ashley's laughter was pure happiness. "It's true love, Mom." Ashley reached for Jessica's hand. Her daughter's face sobered. "And it's all because of you. Thanks for believing in me. For always being there. For your love."

Ashley's face was wavy before her eyes.

Harry reached across the table to touch her arm. "Thank you, Mum. I never would have known happiness or lived my dream without this girl you gave birth to. I love you."

Jessica couldn't help herself. She launched her body in between them, grasping hard. *Thank You, God, for letting my dreams come true.* Jessica had never been happier.

Chapter 16

Ellie sat there in disbelief after Henry slammed the door. She tried to feel him in her heart, but nothing, absolutely nothing.

Sophie was still next to her, a look of confusion on her face. "Did we offend Henry? Why'd he run off?"

Ellie's chest ached. An emptiness in her heart where his presence usually lived. A sudden chill encompassed her. "I don't know. I need to talk to him." Ellie ran out the door to find him, but Henry was nowhere in sight. Their car was gone. She pulled her cell and speed dialed Henry, but it went right to voicemail. She texted him.

> Henry, what's wrong? Are you mad at me? Please talk to me. I love you.

Ellie was having trouble seeing. Was he angry because she'd answered for them? She had correctly read the feelings in his heart, hadn't she?

Sophie and Ben were by her side. Even though they offered words of comfort, it didn't help. The pair followed her home.

Ellie ran in, finding Darcy snuggling with Maggie in the rocking chair.

"Mum, is Henry here?"

Darcy smiled until she caught the desperation in Ellie's eyes. "No, child. What's wrong?"

The words were difficult to get out. "We, we had a fight."

Darcy's eyes widened. "You two? A fight? I don't believe it. About what?"

Ellie shook her head. "It's personal. I've got to find him." Ellie ran out the door. She headed to the office, but he wasn't there. She searched every greenhouse, the barns, everywhere she could think of, but still nothing. Henry was gone.

She jumped when her phone rang. "Henry?"

The voice of Cassandra, her mother, greeted her. "Ellie, what happened? Darcy called and said something's wrong. What's going on, baby?"

"Henry's mad at me and left. I don't understand. I'll call you back later. I want to keep the line open in case he calls."

"Ellie, calm down. Everyone argues from time to time. It'll be all right, I promise you."

Her words were choppy. "We never fight. I don't understand. How could he leave me?"

Cassandra's voice was quiet. "Every marriage has problems from time to time. Henry loves you. There's no doubt about that. I'm sure it's all a big misunderstanding. Here, let me pray with you."

Despite her mother's efforts, Ellie was shell shocked. *This is my fault. I jumped to conclusions.*

Darkness had fallen by the time Ellie opened the door. The door to the house she and Henry had built. A house of love. She fought back a sob. Sophie was waiting for her and wrapped her arms around Ellie.

"I'm sorry, Ellie. We never should have asked. Did you find Henry?"

Ellie pushed her away. "No. I looked everywhere. Can't find him. I don't know what to do."

Sophie pulled her in again, tears wetting Ellie's shirt. "All my fault. I'm so sorry."

No matter what Sophie or Darcy said, nothing helped. His feelings were missing, like they'd disappeared the night he rescued her. When he almost died. Ellie was borderline hysterical.

Darcy brought her baby to her. Ellie nursed the infant as she tried to figure out what to do. Her arms were shaking so badly, Darcy took Maggie back after feeding, and put the little girl to bed. Darcy then helped Ellie to the bedroom.

Darcy brushed the hair from Ellie's eyes. "Know I should mind my business, but when I find my son, I'll take a spoon to his hide. Damned idiot should know better than to treat his wife like this. He's ticked Mum off one time too many."

"M-maybe, maybe it was me. Maybe I did something wrong. But why won't he at least talk to me?"

Darcy dried her tears. "Menfolk are dumb sometimes. Give it time. He'll come around. This I promise you, and I know him. Don't you dare forget how much my son loves you, arse that he is." Her mother-in-law kissed her, tucked her in and turned off the lights.

Ellie's eyes drifted to the traveling LEDs above the bed. The ones Sophie and Margaret had designed into the room. The ones that read, 'Henry loves Ellie loves Henry loves Ellie' in an unending circle. Ellie couldn't take it. She covered her head with Henry's pillow so she didn't have to see them.

***

Edmund opened the door to the Tea Room. The automatic paper towel dispenser in the men's room had quit working. *Probably the batteries.* He had some along and planned on replacing them.

A clanging noise came from the kitchen. Someone was working in the back. Undoubtedly his future sister-in-law, Sophie. Might as well say hello. He pushed the door open to the kitchen and his mouth went dry. It wasn't Sophie standing there. Facing away from him was Ashley. Edmund's heart pounded.

"What are you doing here? I thought you and Harry were going to Penn State to visit Maggot."

She turned to him. *Something's wrong.* "Sophie couldn't make it today and asked me to fill in for her. Harry went by himself."

Sophie? Not here? "Is she sick?"

Edmund had to force himself not to wrap her in his arms when he caught the glimpse of sadness on her face. "She's with Ellie. Something happened between Ellie and Henry. Do you know where Henry is?"

Edmund had come in late last night, after watching a movie with Tara. He no longer spent his nights with her, instead honoring Tara as Henry had suggested. And he'd left before anyone was up. "No. What do you mean, 'where's Henry?'"

Ashley scrubbed a mark on the stove top. She was so beautiful, it pained Edmund to look at her. *Leave, now.*

"They must've had a really bad fight. Henry left and Ellie's beside herself. She couldn't get out of bed. Sophie's with her. I don't understand. They're so in love. What makes men act like idiots?"

Edmund's passion for Ashley was fighting against his self-control. He stared at the floor. *Perfect opportunity. Tell her how you feel!* He forced himself to start backing away. *No! Get thee behind me, Satan.*

The room was silent. He glanced at Ashley. She was studying him with those beautiful eyes, face sporting a frown. "Are you okay?"

Run. "Yeah. Look, don't know what happened. Forgot the batteries to fix the towel paper, I mean paper towel holder right now. I'll go to town and get some. Fix it tomorrow. Bye."

Edmund almost ran out of the shop. He threw open the car door and pounced on the seat. Pain radiated from his hip. He scooped the batteries from his pocket and fired the motor. *Can't do this. She's Henry's girl, and I love Tara. Need to go, now.* The wheels squealed when he gunned the motor. He cast one last glance at the Tea Room, realizing Ashley was standing at the door watching him.

***

Henry's eyes slowly focused. His head was pounding. After rushing from Ben's house, he'd hit the liquor store. An empty whiskey bottle stared back at him from the bedside table. *Where am I?* It all came back. He'd spent the night in a motel on the other side of Lancaster.

Henry forced himself to a sitting position, but the room spun so crazily he fell back onto the covers. His mind replayed the events from last night. And what Ben and Sophie—no, it had to be Sophie—what Sophie had wanted. Sophie, his crazy, demented Italian friend. *Friend? Yeah, right.* The words Ben had said might have well come from Sophie's lips. 'We want you to father our child'.

Damn that girl. Best friend or not, she'd gone over the line this time. Henry's mind drifted back to the evening he wed Ellie. When Sophie floored him by asking why the two of them hadn't become a couple. Of course Ellie had said it was because Sophie was drunk, but he'd suspected more. And then when she started asking for a kiss whenever he kissed Ellie... And Ellie had encouraged it, because 'he and Sophie were best friends'. It was all so plain now. Sophie had a thing for him. *Never saw this coming.* He was so mad at Sophie he could spit tacks.

But that wasn't what angered him the most. He was furious with Ellie. His soulmate, his wife. Without blinking an eye, she'd answered for him. 'We'd be honored for Henry to father your child'. Like he was some damned piece of meat. A prized bull pressed into service to impregnate a heifer. And he'd understood her feelings right away. Ellie wanted him to sleep with Sophie and make her pregnant.

The thought of sleeping with anyone besides his wife sickened him. He forced himself out of bed and stumbled to the bathroom. It wasn't his thoughts, but the liquor that forced the vomit. He wiped his mouth and cleaned up the floor where he'd missed. The room spiraled even faster as he found the bed again.

What am I supposed to do now? He had no desire to break his wedding vows, but Ellie wanted him to. To sleep with Sophie. To father her child.

Two hours later, he'd made up his mind. If that's what his wife wanted, that's what he would do. *You win, Sophie.* Ben's wife had swayed Ellie's mind. *Only one time.* If it doesn't work, forget it.

But the thing that worried him the most was how could he ever see Ellie the same, after this? He checked his hands. They no longer shook. He'd grab some food and a couple more bottles of Scotch. To drown the pain and disappointment in his heart. He grabbed his phone and powered it back on. He fired off a text, then turned it back off.

Make arrangements for us to meet Ben and Sophie – their house – 8PM two days from now. Kiss Maggie for me. Henry.

Henry threw the cell in the corner, found his car keys and stumbled out the door.

Chapter 17

 dmund sat at the table next to Tara, trying his hardest to concentrate on the task at hand, picking out wedding invitations. The close encounter with Ashley earlier in the day had thrown him off kilter.

"Which one do you like best? The one with doves or the two entwined rings?"

It would be easy to tell her to make the selection, but Edmund couldn't. Not after everything he'd put her through. He'd vowed to be a better man, for Tara's sake. *God, I love her.* He forced his attention on the samples. "Doves kind of signify us flying off to a new life together, but I like the rings more. Two lives, joined together in an unending circle. Yes, I like these the best. What do you think?"

Tara didn't answer right away. He caught the moisture in her eye. "Sorry. Did I say something wrong?"

Her arms slowly pulled him toward her. The taste of her lip gloss thrilled him. Did she say it was orange frost? No, it wasn't the taste of the gloss, it was Tara's essence. "You said everything right. I love you so much." Her lips again found his. "Let's head down to the hot tub, what do you think?"

Desire. To hold her, to take her like he'd done so many times before. All of his soul had to pitch in to fight off the passion he had for her. "I really want to wait until our wedding night." Sadness filled his heart. Tara had been right. She'd only been a convenience. Until his eyes were opened from their time apart. *I was such a fool.*

Tara's lips were pouty. "Don't you want me?"

He was losing control. "You know I do, but..." His lips found the hollow of her throat and he kissed her there gently.

"Edmund..."

His breath was hard and fast. "Tara, please. I'm trying to be honorable. To show you love... and respect. Like I should have from the beginning. But you're so irresistible..."

Tara pushed him away. Now she was the one breathing in clumps. "Okay, okay, but you've got to stop this now if we're going to wait."

Edmund retreated to his seat, but his hand held her fingertips. The hands he once thought were too thick for his liking were now the object of his desire. As he kissed her fingertips, she brushed the hair from his eyes.

"I don't know what happened during the time we were apart, but please, stay like this forever." Her eyes were glistening.

"Anything my lady desires."

The fire of passion in her eyes was becoming manageable again. "I've got a crazy idea."

Edmund stifled his laughter. "Why should this one be any different?"

Tara pinched his cheek. "Smarty." Her smile lessened, but still graced her face.

Edmund couldn't help himself. He leaned in for another kiss and languished in her delectable taste. "I love you, Tara. I'll do anything you desire. Just ask."

Her hands were trembling. *Must be exceptionally crazy.*

"What do you think about wearing a traditional Scottish kilt when we get married?"

The idea was so ludicrous that he choked on his own saliva. *A man skirt? I despise those things.* But he could see the look on her face. "If that's what you want, the answer's yes."

Tara's eyes lit up as if they were on fire. "Are you serious? You'd do that for me?"

As much as he despised the idea, it must be important to her, for whatever reason. He had no desire to show his legs in public. That's why he never wore shorts. "Absolutely. I'd wear or do anything for you."

Tara rewarded him with a very warm, wet and prolonged kiss. "Do you mean anything?"

"Of course. Tell me your wishes, my lady."

"I, uh, this may sound weird, but, would you paint my nails tonight?"

What? "Are you serious?"

"Yes. I read a book once where this man painted his fiancée's nails. The scene was so romantic. Would you mind?"

He bit his lips to keep the laughter in. "I may not be good at it, but anything my love desires, it shall be done."

Tara's hands were trembling as she led him to her bedroom.

***

Tara woke alone. *Darn, why'd he have to be so noble?* One glance at her fingernails told her she would need to remove Edmund's attempts and repaint. The smears of pink on her toes looked like a painter's drop cloth.

She giggled out loud. "I'll cut the man a break. Must have been hard with me flirting the way I did." She'd wanted Edmund so badly last night, but as he explained, he'd made a promise to her and would die before breaking it.

She was fifteen minutes late getting to the office. Tracy shot her a frown, then a wink. "Have fun last night, Ms. Miller?"

Fun wasn't the right word. "The stuff of dreams, Tracy." She returned the wink to her friend.

Tara suddenly ran into a solid object and fell backwards to the floor. She glanced up to see the lab-coated man before her, Dr. Joseph Royer. He quickly reached for her hand. "I'm so sorry, Tara. Shouldn't have been standing in the hallway like that."

Her cheeks caught fire. "No, totally my fault. Are you okay?"

He didn't smile as his eyes engaged hers. "Quite all right. You have a funny way about you this morning."

That was confusing. "A funny way about me?"

"Yes. That was a unique way to say good morning."

"Joe, I mean, Dr. Royer, I apologize."

His eyebrows raised. "May I speak with you, privately?"

Spiders were suddenly crawling up her neck. "Uh, sure." She walked into her office and stared in confusion when he closed the door behind him. What happened next floored her. Joe stood in front of her, eyes boring into her soul. His left arm found its way around her waist and he drew her close. His pulse was strong against her skin where his fingers touched her chin as he raised her mouth toward his. The minty smell of his breath mingled with the sweet taste of his lips as they softly joined hers.

Tara closed her eyes and was suddenly on the beach, cool waves providing a direct contrast to the wonderfully warm pleasure of this exciting man's lips against hers. When Joe pulled away, the vision evaporated like a wisp of smoke. The coarseness of his lab coat in her hands drew her attention. Her eyes dropped to the fabric buried in her fists where she'd grasped tightly to pull him close. Tara glanced at his eyes, noting the smolder in his irises. *This can't be happening. I love Edmund.* She quickly pushed him away.

Rohrer was breathing hard. "Sorry. Had to do that one time, just to find out."

Tara backed away from him. "Find out what?"

"If I was making a mistake. If what I felt from you was real." He studied her reaction and bit his lips. "Obviously, I was wrong. My apologies and I guarantee I'll never do that again. My announcement today will be proof of it. Goodbye, Tara."

Rohrer turned and closed the door behind him on his way out. Tara was struggling to gain her composure when a knock sounded on the door.

"C-come in."

Tracy entered. Her eyes grew wide and she immediately shut the door behind her. "What happened in here? Looks like you've seen a ghost."

Tara's hands were trembling. "I, uh, I..."

Tracy nodded knowingly. "I know what happened."

God, no. "W-w-what do you think happened?"

"He told you, didn't he?"

Yes he had, just not in words. "Told me what?"

"About this." Tracy handed her an inter-office memo.

It is with regrets that I announce my departure from the practice. I've joined another office in Leola, closer to my family. I've enjoyed the last two years and will miss the staff and friends I've made here. My resignation is effective today. Dr. Joseph Rohrer.

Tara's hand flew to her mouth. "Oh my God."

Chapter 18

*E*llie was worried about Henry. Ever since they'd met, the two had been able to feel what the other felt, sometimes even being able to read each other's minds. Three nights ago, she'd thought she'd correctly understood what Henry had in his heart... when Ben and Sophie asked if he would be the donor for their child. Since she thought she understood his feelings, she'd answered for both of them. Told the Millers that Henry would gladly father their child.

As soon as the words left her lips, she regretted not talking it over with Henry first. Now, her heart was breaking because she could no longer feel anything, anything at all from her husband.

A cold front was coming in, driving wind and rain before it. Henry's wounds would be bothering him. Bracing against the wind, Ellie walked the short distance to the old house Ben and Sophie had renovated. She rang the doorbell, wondering about Henry's frame of mind when he would arrive.

Sophie answered and hugged her tightly. "Have you heard from Henry?"

Ellie vowed she wouldn't cry, though her nose now tingled. "No, not a word."

"Look, Ellie, I didn't mean to cause problems between you two. It was a stupid idea, my idea. Sorry I brought it up. Let's just forget the whole thing." Sophie wiped her cheeks.

Ellie held her hands. "Soph, you're our best friends. We'll do whatever we can to help you two. I think it was just the shock of it all. Henry will come around, wait and see."

Henry had texted for them to meet at eight, but it was half past when he knocked on the door.

Ben answered. "Henry, there you are. We've been worried sick about you. Please come in and have a seat."

Henry's eyes were icy as he glanced at Ellie and Sophie. "Eleanor. Sophia."

Ben was obviously concerned. "Are you all right, Henry?"

Henry didn't answer. He knew the Miller house intimately, since the two couples were best friends. Henry walked into the dining room and sat down at the table. His lips were pinched together and white. Ellie walked to him, gently taking his hand in hers. Henry immediately yanked it away. Everyone could tell he was upset.

Henry got right down to business. "I thought this over. Here's how it goes. First, the child is never to know I'm the father. Second, the child will not have any part of my name. Third, I'll have nothing to do with him or her, ever. There'll be no special bonding or me being the godfather or anything like that." He turned his eyes to Sophie. "The last thing is, you get one shot at this, Sophie. If it works, fine, if not, we'll never again try this lunacy."

Ellie studied his face. "Whoa, Henry. Why don't we talk about this?"

Henry shoved the chair away from himself as he stood and turned toward Ellie. The expression he gave her was anger, or was it more? "You threw away all opportunity to discuss this insanity when *you* agreed without my input."

Sophie was whimpering. "Henry, why don't you and Ellie take the time to discuss this? The last thing I want to do is cause a problem between the two of you or to jeopardize our friendship. We can..."

Henry's screamed response caused all of them to reel. "Either you want me to help or not. Agree to my terms or I walk out, never to return!"

Ellie's life flashed before her eyes. So many great memories, all of Henry. She touched his shoulder. "You and I need to talk, okay?"

He shoved her hand away. "No. You want me to sleep with her, so I will. We do it right now or I'm out of here."

Sophie's tears rained down in a torrent. Head down, she turned away.

Henry misunderstood. Sleep with Sophie? Never. Ellie began laughing uncontrollably. Ben joined her.

Sophie turned to stare at Henry with tears puddling on the floor. Her whisper was directed to Henry. "You act like I'm some whore to be serviced. I wasn't asking you to sleep with me. I was asking you to donate your semen, so we could have a child. Forget it. I'll find someone else." She turned to walk away before turning back to face him once again. "All these years, I thought you were my best friend. I loved and respected you, thinking you were the greatest man ever born. But after the callous way you just treated me..."

Sophie stumbled and grasped a chair. Ben was immediately at her side.

"I was wrong all this time," Sophie continued. "You're just a stupid, bloody ass. I guarantee you, if I had to sleep with you to have a child, I'd rather be barren throughout eternity. Damn you, Henry Campbell, for turning something so beautiful into vulgarity." Her sobs echoed behind her as she ran from the room.

Henry's mouth dropped open as he stared at her retreating figure. Ellie's laughter had now been replaced by anger. *Henry wanted to sleep with Sophie?* Never in her wildest dreams did she ever think Henry would sleep with any girl, for any reason. *What's wrong with you?* How could Henry be so inwardly focused? Did he realize how much he'd hurt Sophie just now?

Ellie's hands were on her hips as she stared at her husband. Did he really think she wanted him to sleep with Sophie so she could become pregnant? *That explains why you're angry with me.* "You don't have to sleep with her. You place your donation in a collection bottle. The doctor takes over from there."

Henry's face was bright red. He'd obviously misunderstood and was embarrassed. Without looking at either Ellie or Benjamin, he asked when he needed to make this donation. Ben replied that their physician felt Monday or Tuesday would be opportune. They agreed on a time before Henry and Ellie left.

The short walk home was not pleasant. Both were angry. On the doorstep, Ellie turned to her husband. "Were you really going to sleep with her?"

"I was pretty damned sure that was what you wanted."

"How could you even think something like that? What possessed you to—"

He snapped. "I guess I was just shocked that my wife, supposedly my best friend, offered the use of my, my... well, you know what you offered. Like I was a prostitute and you were my pimp."

"Are you an idiot? How could you even think I wanted you to sleep with Sophie? We signed up for faithfulness for life. At least *I* did! What... did the idea of sleeping with Sophie turn you on? Is that it? Did you secretly want her, especially after she told you she was in love with you at our wedding?"

His face was set in stone. "What? No, Eleanor. I never wanted to sleep with anyone but you. But I felt that was what you wanted me to do. And how dare you insinuate that you were the only one wishing for a life of faithfulness? Did you forget that I alone kept looking for you, long after the police said you were dead? I rescued you. I've loved you since before I knew your name, in case you've forgotten."

Ellie's vision was bathed in red. "Right away you have to throw in the fact that you rescued me, some damsel in distress. Admit it. You just happened to be in the right place at the right time. I would have been released and you know it."

Henry was so angry, he didn't say another word. He stormed off into the night.

***

Tara's insides shook to the core. Joe's kiss made her feel... well, she didn't know what it made her feel, except shaky. Her thoughts had been on the sweetness of Joe's lips all day long. Tara needed to put it out of her mind, to calm herself before facing Edmund. *Should I tell him what happened?* No. He'd never understand. Edmund loved her, only her, and would never allow something like that to happen to him. She'd have to hide this. Somehow. Some way. *If I can.*

The path to the door seemed five hundred miles long. The coolness of the metal doorknob stemmed the shaking, well, a little. She slowly swung open the door. The luscious scent of broiled scallops filled the air. Almost before she crossed the threshold, Edmund wrapped his arms around her and embraced her. His lips never tasted as good as they did now. Tara dropped her bag and threw her arms around his neck, snuggling warmly against him.

Edmund pulled away. "Welcome home, my lady."

She had no idea why her cheeks were steamy. "I love you so much, Edmund. Missed you today." Tara gently kissed him time after time. The heat of passion was rising in her chest.

A beeping noise interrupted them. He kissed her nose, then helped her out of her coat. "Dinner's ready. While you wash up, I'll serve the food."

Will he see it in my eyes? He might. "Can we eat by candlelight?"

His smile made her dizzy. "Ooh. *Très romantique ce soir, oui?*"

"Yes, I love you. Do you know that?"

His eyebrows raised. *Can he see it in my eyes?*

He studied her briefly, then a smile slowly spread across his face. "I've never been surer of anything in all my life. Let me find the candles." Edmund turned to search through the kitchen junk drawer.

Never more sure than anything? The way he loves me. Why do I feel so guilty? Can I say the same?

***

Ellie couldn't fall asleep. The traveling LEDs taunted her. 'Henry loves Ellie loves Henry loves Ellie'. *Does he even love me anymore?* Based on the last couple of days, she had her doubts. And what hurt the worst was she couldn't feel him inside of her. She could take it no more.

"I need help." Her mind ran through all the possibilities, but there were really only two. Call her mother or Aunt Kaitlin. Both had worked through problems with their spouses. "Katie's husband was ex-military, just like Henry. Maybe she can help."

She felt bad about the hour; it was already after midnight in Chicago. Her uncle Jeremy answered on the third ring. "Ellie? Everything okay?"

Her throat choked up at the sound of his voice. "Uncle Jeremy, put Aunt Katie on, please?"

"Hold on, kiddo." His voice was muffled. "Katie, wake up. It's Ellie. I think something's wrong."

Kaitlin sounded groggy. "Ellie? What's going on?"

"Henry. Henry left me."

"What?"

"He, he left me."

Kaitlin's voice was no longer groggy. "Tell me what happened, from the beginning."

Ellie downloaded everything, in detail. Kaitlin listened intently. After Ellie finished, Kaitlin was silent for a moment longer. Ellie knew her aunt was thinking. Kaitlin was the smartest person Ellie had ever known.

Kaitlin's voice was soft. "I never told you this, but the same thing happened to Jeremy and me... before we were married."

What? "Someone wanted Jeremy to father their baby?"

"No. Not that part. Jeremy left me. We had a big misunderstanding. When he was hurt, I made the decision to send him back to Chicago, without consulting him. We had this big, horrible fight and he left. I thought we were over for good. I was so scared I could hardly breathe."

"W-what'd you do?"

"I called your mother first, then my mama. She had Aunt Tina and Papaw meet Jeremy at the airport. Calmed him down enough until he and I could talk out our problem, logically."

"But I don't even know where Henry is. He won't answer my calls. He won't respond to my texts. Katie, I'm so worried. Suppose he left for good? My world would be over." The ever changing hues of the LEDs above the bed caught her attention. "I won't be able to stay here, not if I want to keep my sanity. Where would I go?"

Katie's voice was soft on the other end of the line. "Honey, if it comes to that, our home is always open to you, and Maggie. We love you, Ellie. You'll always be welcome to stay with us."

Ellie was so grateful for her aunt. "I know you love me. That's why I called. Love both of you, too."

Jeremy's voice came on. "Henry's a good man, Ellie. He'll come around, just give him a couple of days. It'll be fine. But, if you want me to come find him and talk some sense into the man, say the word and both of us are on the next plane."

Ellie nodded, then realized they couldn't see her reaction. "Might take you up on that. Thanks to both of you. Sorry to wake you up. I just needed a friendly voice. 'Night."

The LEDs were still rotating on the ceiling. Mocking her. But knowing she wasn't alone helped... a little. Henry's face floated before her. She reached out into the night, feeling for him. Nothing. *Where are you, sweetheart? Do you even care?*

Chapter 19

"*I* made apple crisp. Do you think Mum will like it?" Ashley was so excited. Today was Darcy's birthday and the whole family, well, hopefully the whole family, would be there.

Harry's laughter drifted over from the driver's seat of the new car they'd picked out. *No, the one I picked out.* Harry had insisted she be the one to choose the vehicle and every option. He'd also insisted on the title being in her name, though she couldn't drive, yet. Harry promised to teach her.

The whole experience had been fun, except for the part when Harry lost his temper over the way the salesman had joked with her. Harry had insisted they change to a saleswoman. His voice broke into her thoughts.

"Mum will love it. She'll ask for the recipe and want you to make it with her sometime." He cleared his throat. "Now, when we get there, Edmund and I have an errand to run."

Suddenly cold, she shivered. "It has something to do with Henry, doesn't it?"

"Yes, princess, it does. He won't answer Ellie's calls or texts. She has no idea where he is. Mum made it clear that she expects Henry to be there today, so we're going to get him."

"But if Ellie doesn't know where he is, how will you find him?"

Harry grunted. "Edmund figured out how. He called the credit card company. Pretended he was Henry and asked them to review his recent transactions. That's how we know where he's staying."

"I see. Suppose he doesn't want to come?"

Harry's jaw was firmly set. "He'll come willingly or I'll drag him. Can't believe he's treated Ellie like this. She doesn't deserve it. Don't know what happened, but my sister-in-law is beside herself."

Ashley reached for his hand. So tough, yet warm and filled with kindness. *I can feel your love.* An observation she'd made interrupted her thought. "Whatever it is, I think it involves Sophie. She hasn't been at the Tea Room for days. I went to see her and she wouldn't stop crying." She studied his face for a reaction. "You don't think Sophie and Henry were... you know..."

Harry shook his head violently. "No. That's not even a remote possibility. Henry loves Ellie. Even though he and Sophie are close, he wouldn't. He couldn't. Not my brother."

"But he kisses Sophie all the time. On the lips."

"They're friends, princess. Only friends. Have been for almost a decade. And Ellie's apparently okay with it."

Ashley was still confused about that. "So it's all right for a man to kiss a lady friend on the lips?"

Harry was momentarily silent. "I guess so. If your wife allows it."

It was Ashley's turn to be quiet. "Do you ever kiss other girls?"

Harry laughed and turned his head to her. The love in his eyes was so apparent, she could almost touch it. "You, my love, are the only girl I've *ever* kissed on the lips."

"Not even Ellie?"

He scratched his chin. "Of course not. She's Henry's wife. Besides, I only want to kiss you. How about you? Ever kissed another man?"

Ashley turned to look out the window. If she told Harry the truth, he'd be furious. Even if it was four years ago. Sam Espenshade had kissed her once, when she'd been really sick. On Valentine's Day. And she dare not breathe a word about how Edmund had tried to kiss her at the picnic. She shivered as she lied to her fiancé. "Nope. I saved all my kisses for you."

They were at a stop sign. "Then, let me taste your lips again." Big, tough Harry was so gentle when his lips touched hers. His scent was scrumptious.

At Ellie's house, gentleman Harry held both the car and house doors for her. Margaret, Tara and Darcy were talking in the dining room as they entered. All three took turns hugging her. Ellie's eyes were vacant as she stumbled into the kitchen, holding Maggie. Darcy took the baby so Ellie could hug Ashley.

Ellie clung to her tightly. "Missed you so much, Ash."

"I missed you, too."

Edmund appeared, taking in the scene. He barely glanced at Ashley. "Ready, Harry?"

Harry nodded. "Yeah. Let's go."

The two brothers headed out the door, men on a mission. Would they be successful in bringing Henry back? Ashley hoped so. The house sure didn't feel like a home without Henry.

***

Bang, bang, bang. *What's that incessant noise?* Henry tried to lift his head, but the spinning wouldn't stop. The banging continued. *Must be housekeeping, here to make up the room.*

Henry tried to get out of bed, but his legs didn't support him. Henry's fall upset the end table, the forest of empty whiskey bottles clinking as they cascaded down on top of him. "Go away! I don't want the room cleaned."

But it wasn't the housekeeper's voice that came through the door. It was Harry. "Henry, it's your brothers. Open the door. We need to talk."

My brothers? Ellie must have sent them. "Be gone. I don't want to talk. Leave me alone."

Harry's voice, again. "Open the door, now, before I'm forced to take drastic action."

Drastic action? How dramatic. Henry started to laugh, but it triggered a chain reaction that resulted in jack hammers pounding in his head. "Get out of here and leave me be."

"Fine. Have it your way." The knocking ceased.

Henry wanted to crawl back into bed, but couldn't figure out how.

Damn you, Ellie. Okay, he'd misread her feelings about sleeping with Sophie. *That blunder's on me.* But when he tried to tell her he'd loved her forever and remind her he'd rescued her from the kidnappers, she'd made a fool of him. What was wrong with that woman? *I don't even know my own wife anymore.* He'd wanted to continue the argument, but his pride wouldn't allow it in front of the family or his baby. That left him with one option, to drink his sorrows away. Ellie acted like rescuing her was nothing. He'd nearly died saving her. *Ungrateful little...*

Voices in the corridor caught his attention.

A woman's voice. "I'm not comfortable with this."

"Ma'am, Henry Campbell is our brother. He has a medical condition and we need to make sure he's okay."

Her voice carried a stern tone. "I'll open the door, then ask him if what you said is true. If it's not, I'm calling the police."

"That's acceptable. Just open the door. We're worried about him."

The electric snap of the latch drew his attention. His brothers and a lady walked in. He recognized the woman, the one who'd checked him in. "Mr. Campbell, are you okay?"

Henry wished the floor would quit rocking. "Yes, leave me alone."

"Are these your brothers?"

"Unfortunately, yes."

She eyed him strangely. "Do you need an ambulance? Your brothers said you have a medical condition."

"I don't have a medical condition."

Harry walked over and stared down at him. "Yes, you do. It's called *stupidity*."

The woman eyed all three of them. "I don't know about this. Maybe I should call 911. He looks ill."

Edmund picked up several of the empty liquor bottles. "He's not sick, he's drunk. Drunk as a skunk."

"Mr. Campbell, would you like me to call the police or an ambulance?"

"No, no. It's fine. Just let me be."

"Okay, if you say so." She closed the door behind her.

He turned to face his siblings. "What the hell are you two doing here?"

"Know what today is?"

Henry had no clue what date, or even day of the week it was. "Why should I care?"

Both brothers grabbed his arms and sat Henry on the bed. Harry grabbed his shoulders and shook him. Harry's breath was on his cheeks, but which of the three faces was really his? "It's Mum's birthday, you fool. She sent us to get you." The shaking made his head pound worse.

Henry tried to shove Harry away, but he may as well have tried to push a mountain out of his way. Harry was solid and immovable. "Get away from me."

"You're coming with us. Edmund brought some coffee. Let's get you in the shower. That will help."

Anger filled his vision. "Stop telling me what to do!" Henry took a swing at Harry, but missed. Henry landed on the floor.

A wicked laugh came from his brother. "Okay, have it your way." Within seconds, Harry stripped off his clothes, grabbed him by the hair and arm and yanked him into the bathroom. Harry flung him into the tub.

The flowing icy cold water chilled his body, but inflamed his temper. "Damn you. Turn off the water. So help me, when I get my hands on you..."

Harry grabbed his hair and held his face under the shower head. Henry had to spit out the water to keep from drowning. Harry's grip was too firm to break away. His younger brother roughly scrubbed him from head to toe, forcing him to remain under the icy flow for what seemed to be an eternity.

Henry was shaking uncontrollably from the freezing water. Harry grasped him under the arms and unceremoniously deposited him on the bed. His brother threw a towel at him. "Dry yourself off and get dressed. Or maybe you want me to do that too, drunkard."

Henry could handle himself in a fight any day, except today. He wanted one, but the redness of Harry's three faces made him reconsider.

"Edmund, do you have the coffee ready for Henry?"

Edmund? Where had he come from? He was holding a cup. "Yes. Please drink this, Henry."

"I don't want any..."

Henry didn't get a chance to finish. Harry grabbed his nose and chin to force Henry's mouth open.

Edmund's eyes were kind. "Sorry, brother." Edmund poured some of the lukewarm black coffee down his throat. Henry started choking.

Harry laughed. "Want to drink it on your own now? Or shall I continue to force feed you?"

Henry held his shaking hands in front of him. "No, no. I'll do it."

His brothers backed away, but Harry made sure he drank all four cups before letting him stop.

Harry scooped the clothes from the floor. The same ones he'd worn for days. Harry threw them on the bed next to him. "Put these on, now, before I lose my temper."

"I hate you, Harry."

"Not as much as I hate you right now. Bloody imbecile."

It took a while for Henry to get them on. The pain in his head had reached jet engine level. Edmund handed him some pills and a cup of water. "Chew these. They'll help."

Henry did as he was told. "Why are you here again?"

Edmund's voice was soft. Very kind of him since the slightest noise sounded like an atomic bomb. "We're taking you home. To see Mum. It's her birthday."

Harry wasn't as considerate. He was almost yelling. "And to see your wife, you miserable excuse for a man."

***

It was almost two. Ellie's nerves were shot. An hour ago, she'd felt Henry for the first time in days. Feelings of bitterness and anger. She looked at Darcy, who was studying her. "Mum, I'm not sure I can do this."

Both Tara and Ashley hugged her. Compassion could easily be seen on Darcy's face. "This must be done, child. Need to get it all behind you. It'll be fine, I promise you that. No path in life, not even a great marriage, is always smooth. We're all here for you."

Ellie fought back a sob. *Don't know if I can face him. He's so mad at me.*

The door to the house flew open. Edmund and Harry stood on either side of Henry, lugging him in.

Ellie's chest ached when she saw him. *He looks horrible.*

The look of anger on Henry's face matched the feelings that were emanating from him. No matter, Ellie's heart went out to him.

Edmund pulled out the chair next to her and Harry slammed him into it. Edmund pushed the chair in. Henry shot everyone icy glances, except Ellie. He didn't even look at his wife.

Harry's voice was firm, but calm. "What do you have to say to Mum?"

Henry didn't answer right away. Harry shook him from behind.

"Stop that. I have a headache."

"No, brother. You're hungover. What do you have to say to Mum?"

"Happy birthday, Mum."

"Thanks, son." Darcy glanced around the table, then smiled. "So good to have the family with me on my twenty-ninth birthday." Her comment brought laughter from everyone but Ellie and Henry. It was plain as the nose on her face Henry didn't want to be there.

Henry turned and glared at Ellie.

Darcy caught the exchange. "That's it. I need help in the kitchen." Everyone except Henry and Ellie stood, but Darcy's voice stopped them cold. "I want Ellie and Henry to help me. In the kitchen, now. Everyone else, sit."

Reluctantly, the two of them followed Henry's mother into the kitchen. Ellie tried to help her husband, but he pulled away, stumbling after the two women.

The door was barely closed when Darcy turned and spoke sternly. "I've had about enough of this bloody crap from both of you. I don't know what transpired, but get past it." Ellie couldn't look at her face. "This home has always been full of joy, because of the love you two have for each other. Ever since whatever happened, it's no longer a home. It's just a house of stone, bricks and mortar. Now you two work out your issues right now or I'm heading back to Scotland in the morning, permanently. I did not move three thousand miles to watch the two of you act like prissy, spoiled little lassies. For Heaven's sake, you two love each other. Did you forget that?"

Darcy wiped her mouth.

"Let me tell you," she continued her rant. "I wish every day that your pop was still here with me. I miss him so much. And seeing you two carry on like this breaks my heart. What a waste."

Neither looked at her.

Darcy shook her head. "By damn, you're idiots. I'd gladly take what you two have instead of watching you piss it away. I'm going back to the table and wait five minutes to say grace. If you're not out by then, to hell with both of you." With that, she stormed out of the kitchen.

It took a moment before their eyes met. Henry was the first to speak. "You hurt me, Ellie."

"You hurt me, too, Henry."

He silently stared for a moment before dropping his eyes to the floor. "I know. Acted like a fool, didn't I?"

"Yes, you did." She lifted his chin. "But so did I. Wish I could take back every unkind word I said to you. I apologize that I answered Ben and Sophie without talking to you first and I really, really regret saying what I did about you rescuing me. I was cruel."

Henry rubbed his hands over his face. "No, I was the cruel one. Please forgive me. I shouldn't have put my feelings before yours. Shouldn't have treated you like you were nothing." He swallowed, hard. "You're everything to me. Any possible way you can forgive me?"

Ellie brushed her eyes and nodded. Henry opened his arms. She fell into his embrace and they clung to each other tightly.

"Only on one condition, Henry."

"What's that?"

"If you forgive me first."

Henry's kiss was so sweet. Her happiest moment in almost a week. "Done. I love you, Ellie."

She pulled back. "I love you, too, but there's one more thing to do."

His blurry eyes showed confusion. "What's that?"

"Go see Sophie. She's so upset she can't even get out of bed."

Henry nodded. "Okay."

They were holding hands when Ellie pushed open the door to the dining room. Ellie smiled at the collective sigh of relief. But the best thing was the feeling flowing from Henry toward her once more. His love for her.

Darcy slammed into them, suffocating them with her hug. "Blessed be the Lord. I hated the thought of packing. Now we can finally celebrate my birthday, as a happy family."

***

Henry stood outside the Miller's door. A house he knew well because of their close friendship. He'd begged Ellie to come with him, but she'd told him this was one journey he'd have to make on his own.

His arm throbbed. A chill was in the air. The seasons were changing. He shivered, from the cold or his cruelty? Ben answered his knock. Sophie's husband looked haggard.

"Henry. How be you?"

"Feeling like a fool. Need to apologize for the way I acted."

Ben studied him. "You and El get everything squared away?"

Henry's eyes concentrated on the porch floor. "Yes. Took a family intervention, but we're good."

Henry was surprised when Ben grabbed him in a tight hug. "That's great. I was worried about the two of you."

His eyes were suddenly scratchy. "May I speak with Sophie?"

"Sure, come on in." Ben led him up the stairs, to the room he shared with his wife. Ben knocked on the door. "Sophie?"

Henry's heartstrings were pulled at the sound of her voice. She'd obviously been crying. "What do you want, Benjy?"

Ben opened the door. "You have a visitor."

Henry stepped across the threshold. Sophie was wrapped in her blankets. Her hair was askew and her eyes were puffy and red. "Hi, Sophie."

Sophie pulled her knees to her chest. "Make him leave. He's not welcome in our home anymore."

Ben sat next to his wife. "Yes, he is. Henry's your best friend."

"Was. Get out of here, Henry. I never want to see your face again."

Ben kissed her forehead. "Just listen to him. I'll be in the hallway if you need me, but the two of you should talk."

Sophie didn't look comfortable after Ben left. She pulled the covers up to her chin and stared at the wall. "What do you want?"

"To tell you I'm sorry. For treating you so horridly. I wish I could take everything back and do it all over again."

Her eyes met his. Sorrow overflowed onto her cheeks. "But you can't. Your actions told me how you really felt about me. And all this time I thought..." She buried her head in her hands. Her shoulders shook as she sobbed.

Henry sat next to her and tried to hold her in his arms. "Sophie, I'm..."

The suddenness of her slap startled him. "I hate you." She followed through with another.

I deserved that. He pulled her to him. "I understand you're upset, but I love you. I'll do anything to make it up to you."

She tried to push him away, but he wouldn't let her. He held her tightly. "I'm so sorry. I regret treating you that way."

Sophie viciously pinched his arm, the bad one. Henry immediately released her. "But you did, and I hate you for it." Her moist eyes sought his. "I can't believe this. For years, we were so close and then..."

Henry nodded as he rubbed the scar on his arm. "I'm an ass. I came over to beg your forgiveness."

Her voice mocked him. "Forgiveness for what, Henry?"

"For being a fool. I hope someday you'll forgive me."

Sophie stared at him and shook her head. Her chin was trembling. Henry placed his hands on the bed, preparing to exit.

His friend grasped him so tightly he could barely draw a breath. "How could I possibly hate you when I love you so much?" He could feel her breath against his ear when she whispered, "I love you, but treat me like that again and I'll sack you for good."

Sophie pulled away. Henry held her head and dried her cheeks with his thumbs. "I promise I'll never take you or our friendship for granted again. Can you forgive me?"

She nodded and again hugged him tightly. "Of course I forgive you. I hope you know what you mean to me."

Why does she care so much? They'd always been close, but still...

Sophie whispered in his ear, "Make it up to me."

Please, no. Every hair on his body stood on end. "How?"

She now grasped his head so their noses were touching. "Get Ellie and let's go celebrate our friendship. Go out one last time before I get pregnant. Won't be able to drink then, but I sure do need one now."

Henry breathed a sigh of relief. Partly because she'd left him off the hook, partly because their friendship wasn't destroyed, but also because of fear of what he'd prayed she wouldn't ask for. Something he'd never do, friend or not.

"Can we possibly go out tomorrow? Haven't seen much of Ellie or Maggie for the last week. That okay?"

Sophie kissed his cheek. "Yes." She held his head again so they were eye to eye. "Please don't ever jeopardize our friendship again. Felt like I was dying inside. Don't you ever forget how much I need you. Now go home and give Ellie a kiss for me." Sophie released him.

Henry stood, curious about the look of joy on Sophie's face. *What do I really mean to her?* He pondered that all night.

Chapter 20

*T*he scent of freshly brewed hibiscus tea filled the room. So fragrant... absolutely wonderful, just like her life. Ashley poured a cup, then walked to sit at a table in the Tea Room. It was a couple of hours before the guests would arrive. Everything was elegantly decorated for the season. In the corner stood a gigantic tree she and Harry had decorated. Next year, they'd decorate their own tree, in their own home.

Ashley ran the Tea Room these days. Ever since Sophie found out she was pregnant, her soon to be sister-in-law was solely focused on preparing the nursery. Ashley quickly wiped away a tear for the children she'd never have, but Harry repeated that it didn't matter. If they wanted children down the road, they'd adopt.

Ellie rarely stopped by anymore. So busy being a mother, wife and friend. Ashley had witnessed Ellie and Henry draw closer after their big argument. Ashley and Harry spent a lot of time with them. *Always wanted a big, happy family.* Now she had one. And Harry made it a point of including her mother in almost all things.

Ashley walked over and straightened one of the wreaths on the window. She smiled. Hard to believe her mom had started dating. It felt a little weird going on a double date with her mom, but last night had been fun. Jessica's date thought she and Ashley were sisters and neither told him different.

The man treated them to the first hockey game she'd ever seen. Harry liked hockey and got really excited when some player named Mickey Campeau scored a hat trick, whatever that was. Ashley giggled as she remembered everyone throwing their hats onto the ice.

Her mom was wonderful, helping with the wedding preparations. Last weekend, they'd ordered her wedding gown. *Me, a bride.* Their wedding day—Valentine's Day—was only a few weeks away. She and Harry were going apartment hunting tonight. *Still can't believe my dreams came true.*

A blowing horn from a passing car caught her attention. The woman inside waved as she drove past. *Tara. My sister.* Forget the in-law part. Tara and Ashley were best friends now. Ashley emptied the rest of her brew.

The only dark spot was Edmund, and how he treated her. So distant. He despised her and she didn't have a clue why. Ashley always tried to be nice to him, but Edmund avoided her like the plague. Ashley was pondering that when the bell on the door rang. Edmund.

He stopped and his face paled. Probably here to replace that stupid paper towel dispenser. It broke down every time the shop was busy.

He held a carton in front of him. Edmund was wearing his handyman's tool belt. He nodded at her. "Ashley."

His tone wasn't friendly, but her mom had said to be kind to people, regardless of how they treated you. "Morning, Edmund. How are you today?"

"Uh, great. Replacing that clunker of a dispenser. Be out of your hair shortly."

"Not in my hair. Want a cup of tea?"

"Uh, no. Be done shortly." He headed into the men's room.

Why doesn't he like me? They'd see each other quite often over the years, being sister and brother-in-law and such. She walked back into the kitchen. Her mother's words rang in her ears. Always show kindness. Ashley poured him a cup of tea. While she'd never personally served him, she knew he liked three lumps of brown sugar in his cup.

Ashley carried his tea into the men's room. He was on his knees, screwdriver in hand. "I know you said no, but I brought you a cup anyway."

Edmund jumped up, dropped the screwdriver and placed his hands on the wall. His face turned white. "You scared the dickens out of me. Don't ever sneak up on me again." He turned his eyes to the cup. "Thanks. Place it on the shelf and be... be on your way."

This was bull crap. Time to get it out in the open. "Why don't you like me?"

He pulled at the neck of his work shirt with his finger. "Never said I didn't."

"Then why do you avoid me?"

"Ashley, I really don't want to get into this with you."

His action angered her. "Well, I want to discuss it. In a few short weeks, we'll be related. I need to know. Answer me. Why don't you like me?"

He backed as far away from her as he could. "Please, Ashley, no."

She walked forward until she was face to face with him. "Does this have something to do with the company picnic, when you tried to kiss me and I refused?"

"No, no. Please leave. I, uh, need to use the toilet."

"Oh, you have to go?"

"Yes, please."

"How bad?"

"Really, really bad."

Ashley poked his chest with her finger. "Okay. I'll leave. As soon as you answer me."

Edmund shrank further into the corner. Ashley stepped forward, her face inches from his.

"Do you hate me?"

"Absolutely not."

"Then why do you treat me like this?"

"Because."

"Because why?"

His breathing was rapid, but his voice was barely a whisper. "Because you belong to Harry."

"So? We can't go on forever like this. Please talk to me. I want us to be close."

"So do I." He placed his hand over his mouth, as if he'd said something he didn't mean.

"So you like me?"

Edmund closed his eyes tightly as if in pain. "Yes, very, *very* much."

Ashley's eyes widened. Did she read him right? "Just how much?"

"Please stop this. I'm trying to be good and honorable. Trying to be a real man."

"What does that have to do with me?" She couldn't quite understand this, but a thought flashed through her mind. It slipped out before she could stop it. "Good heavens. Is it more than liking me?"

Edmund was breathing rapidly. "If I tell the truth, will you stop this?"

What? "Okay. I will."

"Promise? And by promise, I mean no one, especially Harry can ever know."

"I promise."

"Ashley, I'm in love with you. All I can think about is you, your pretty face, your voice and everything about you. In my eyes, you're perfect. I know it's wrong, but I can't help it. Since I can't control myself, I've stayed away from you."

Ashley's mouth fell open. "Y-you're in love with me?"

"Forgive me. Just can't help myself." Edmund wrapped his arms around her. His lips found hers.

Ashley didn't know what to do. His lips felt so good. Her arms wrapped themselves around him and she kissed him back. *Wait! What am I doing?* She pushed him away. *No, no, this is wrong.* "Edmund, we can't continue to do this."

A voice from behind her made her hair stand on end. "But you already did it, didn't you?" In fear, she turned to stare at the face before her. A face filled with rage and murder. Harry.

***

Ellie and Sophie were pulling into the Tea Room lot. Harry was just ahead of them. He waved before he walked in.

"Think Ashley will like it?" The special embroidered handkerchief they'd bought for the wedding had arrived and they couldn't wait to give it to her.

Sophie was all smiles. "She'll love it."

They'd just entered when they heard Ashley's scream coming from the men's room.

"No, no. Don't do it. Please stop!"

Chills ran down Ellie's spine. She turned to Sophie. "Call Henry!" Ellie burst into the room. She couldn't believe the sight. Harry had Edmund's arm over the corner of the sink and was applying weight.

Edmund was begging. "Harry, for the love of God, stop it!" A loud snap resonated through the enclosed area. The sound of Edmund's bone breaking was eclipsed by Edmund's scream.

Ashley pulled at Harry's arm. He flung her into the corner and then grasped Edmund by the collar.

Edmund was crying out in pain. "No, no. Wasn't what you think."

"Does your arm hurt, brother? Don't worry. I'll put you out of your misery. Gonna break your filthy neck!" Harry grasped Edmund's neck and squeezed.

Before Ellie could respond, Ashley flung herself onto Harry and sank her teeth into his arm. Harry threw her off, dropped Edmund and turned toward

Ashley briefly before returning his attention to his brother.

Ellie jumped between Harry and Edmund. "Harry. Stop it! Right now!"

Harry's face had never been so red. Ellie could almost smell his anger. "Move now, Ellie. I don't want to hurt you by mistake."

Ellie touched his raised arm. "If you want to hurt him, you'll have to hit me first."

She saw the tears in Harry's eyes. His arm trembled beneath her touch. Harry backed away and scraped his cheeks. His breath was hard and quick. He turned to stare at Edmund. "God help you, Edmund. Ellie saved your life today, but I swear to God... next time I see you, I will kill you."

Ashley tried to reach for Harry, but Ellie grasped the girl in her arms.

Harry directed his attention at Ashley. "And you, you little tramp." He raised his voice high as if imitating Ashley: *"I save all my kisses for you."* His eyes darkened further. "Except the ones you give my brother, right? Stay away from me. As far as I'm concerned, you no longer exist."

Harry turned, but Sophie was standing in the door, hands in front of her. "Harry, please calm down."

"Move, woman. It's not you I want to hurt." He gently stepped around Sophie before running from the room.

Ellie and Sophie shared an exasperated look. "Did you reach Henry?"

"He's on his way."

Ellie turned to Edmund, who was writhing on the floor, holding his broken arm. She fell to her knees beside him. "Stop moving. Let me see." Edmund was biting his lips, trying not to cry.

Ashley yelled, "Harry, wait! I love you."

Sophie corralled her friend. "Not now. He's too angry."

The door flew open so quickly, Ellie screamed. But it wasn't Harry returning to finish the job. It was Henry. "What in the blazes happened?"

Ellie could only get one word out. "Harry."

***

Ellie watched the telephone poles fly by. Sophie was driving forty miles over the speed limit on the way to the emergency room. Ashley was crying incoherently on the front seat. Ellie had forced her to ride along. Ashley protested, but Ellie refused to allow the girl out of her sight until Henry confronted Harry.

Edmund was whimpering from the pain. "I need an aspirin or something."

"Sorry. They'll give you something at the hospital."

Ellie dialed Tara's office. "This is Ellie Campbell. I need to speak with Tara Miller, right away. It's an emergency."

Edmund's voice was high. "Please, don't tell her."

"I've got to. You can't hide a broken arm and..."

Tara's voice came on the other end. Ellie could sense the fear. "Ellie? What's wrong?"

Edmund was shaking his head 'no'. Ashley had told Ellie what happened. This was something Edmund and Tara would have to work through. "Tara, sorry to bother you. Edmund's had an... an accident."

"Oh God. Is he hurt?"

"He broke his arm, badly. We're on our way to the Emergency Room."

"I'll meet you there. Tell Edmund I love him."

Ellie dropped the cell on her lap.

"What did she say?"

"She said to tell you she loves you."

Edmund's face screwed up. He turned to face the door.

A wailing noise came from behind them. A police siren. Sophie gunned the motor.

"Sophie, no. Pull over. They'll help us."

As soon as the SUV stopped, Ellie was out, hands up and fingers spread. "Officer. We have a medical emergency."

The policeman approached slowly. "On your knees! Hands where I can see them and don't move."

Ellie complied. "His arm. It's badly broken. And the swelling, he has internal bleeding. We need to get him to the hospital."

A second police car slalomed to a stop in front of their vehicle. The officer exited and screamed for Sophie to get out. Sophie did and dropped to her knees next to Ellie.

Ellie pleaded. "Please, look for yourself."

The second officer kept his attention trained on Ellie and Sophie while the first leaned into the door frame. He jumped back out and hollered at the second officer. "No time for an ambulance. We'll escort them. I'll lead, you follow."

Under police escort, the three vehicles sped down the old Philadelphia Pike.

***

Henry entered the emergency department, looking for his wife. Sophie hailed him. "They're in the back. I was waiting for you."

A triage nurse led the pair down the hallway to the room. Sophie clung to Henry's arm. The woman folded the curtain for them. "They're in here."

Ellie sat holding a weeping Ashley on her lap, like a little child. Henry breathed a sigh of relief. *Thank You for protecting my wife.*

Ashley glanced at Henry before burrowing deeper against Ellie. The poor girl's shoulders were heaving.

"Are you okay, honey?"

"I'm fine. You find Harry?"

"No, searched for him everywhere. Looks like he packed and left. His truck is gone." Henry didn't tell her about what he'd found in the greenhouse or Harry's room. Every single one of Harry's prized gladiolas had been pulled out and the bulbs stomped to pieces, blossoms wilting on the floor. In his room, his trunk lid was ajar. Dozens of books had been ripped apart, paper strewn everywhere. His cell was on the bed. Every picture frame of Ashley smashed to smithereens.

"The police gave us an escort. Edmund refused to press charges. Said it was his fault, not Harry's."

"What exactly happened?"

Ashley sat up straight. "Not Edmund's fault, it's mine. He came to fix something and I forced him to tell me why he didn't like me."

Henry could feel the concern coming from Ellie. They shared a worried look.

"I forced him to tell me what was wrong. H-he confessed he was in love with me. Then he kissed me. I-I... uh... kissed him back. That's when Harry walked in. He was so mad." She jumped up and ran to Henry, grabbing his shirt. "You've got to find him. I need to tell him I made a mistake. I didn't mean to kiss Edmund. I love Harry. Edmund wouldn't have kissed me if I hadn't forced him to talk."

Another voice startled all of them. "Edmund told you he was in love with you?" It was Tara. "And he kissed you?"

"Yes, but it was my fault, not his."

Tara's face turned from white to red before their eyes. "But *he* kissed *you*. Did I hear that correctly?"

"I'm sorry, Tara, don't be mad at him."

In front of all of them, Tara pulled her engagement ring from her hand. "He said he could have any woman he wanted. Then he said he'd changed. Edmund lied. Well he's not the only one with options."

Henry shared a look with Ellie. "What did you say, Tara?"

She coldly handed her ring to Henry. "It doesn't matter. Tell your brother to put this somewhere the sun doesn't shine."

Tara turned and left them standing there.

Chapter 21

The pounding of the waves against the beach filled Harry's ears. But the only sound he heard was Ashley's voice yelling after him. The last words he'd ever hear her say. *'I love you.'* And what were his last words to her? *'You no longer exist.'*

San Diego. About as far away from Paradise as you could get. On the beach, people were frolicking, laughing, and having the time of their lives. Such joy. *I'll never be happy again.* He kicked the sand.

His mind drifted to the phone call he'd made to Margaret last night. It was the first time he'd contacted anyone back East. Valentine's Day was supposed to have been a day of happiness. Yesterday, he would have married Ashley, if he'd only acted like a man, instead of a madman.

"Hello?"

"Maggot. It's your brother, Harry."

"Harry, oh my God. How are you? Where are you?"

"None of that's important. How's everyone? Start with Edmund."

"He had to have surgery to pin his bones back together. He just got his cast off yesterday. By the way, Tara called off the engagement when she found out what happened. Edmund's miserable. He misses his brother."

"Yeah, right. When you see him, tell him I'm sorry."

"No, you should do that."

"How's Henry and Ellie? And precious Maggie May?"

"They're fine. Maggie doesn't understand. Every time the door opens, she looks for you."

"Kiss her for me. How's Mum?"

"Heartbroken. Misses you and doesn't comprehend what happened. Why don't you come home?"

"I will. But only long enough to get a few things. I'm... I'm going away, permanently."

Margaret's voice was higher. *"Harry, please don't. We need you. It's not home without you."*

Harry had to force the lump from his throat. *"Just not my home anymore. Neither's Scotland. Decided to join the merchant marine. Shipping out soon. The sea's my new home."*

"Harry, you can't."

"Let's not talk about it. Ashley? How is she?"

The silence that followed chilled him to the core. *"She and her mom had a bad fight on New Year's Day. Ashley left and no one knows where she went. Come home and find her. She loves you, Harry."*

"No, she doesn't. In my anger, I treated her like she was nothing. Can barely live with myself for what I did. So ashamed." Harry started to break

down. *"Gotta go, now. Best sister ever. Always remember I love you."* He'd disconnected before she could answer.

Harry rubbed his eyes and headed back to his old truck. Time to drive back to Paradise. Time to say farewell to his family, forever.

Before him walked a slight, young girl, with thick, wild blonde hair. Harry's mouth dried. Could it be? *Ashley?* He ran to the girl and spun her around. Definitely not Ashley. The girl gave him a dirty look before she walked away.

Harry yelled after her, "Sorry. Thought you were someone I once knew." *And still love with all my heart.*

He opened the door to his pickup. If he breathed deep enough, he could still smell gladiolas, Ashley's scent. Her memory lived there, and haunted him continuously. He slammed the door shut, the door of his personal prison cell.

***

Tara smiled at the man sitting across from her, Dr. Joseph Rohrer. They'd been dating for almost a month now.

"You look lovely tonight, Tara."

He was so amazing. Flowers for each date. The little cards he sent her. How her knees weakened when he kissed her. But something was missing. She bit her lip.

"What's on your mind?"

He'd obviously picked up on her sadness. "Nothing."

The touch of his hand was soothing. His skin soft, like a baby's. So different than Edmund's had been. Rough, calloused... and so incredibly exciting.

"I'm glad I called you a couple weeks ago."

"Me, too."

"Can I ask a question, Joe?"

His eyes crinkled. Just like Edmund's. A warmth stirred in her heart. She was sure it was love, but for who?

His voice got her attention. "Yes, if I can ask one in return."

"Okay. I'll go first. Why'd you leave the practice so quickly? I know you said it was so you could be closer to your family in Leola, but I don't think that was the truth. What was it?"

Joe's eyes didn't leave hers. "I couldn't stand seeing you every day, knowing that the woman I love would never be mine."

Tara's cheeks heated. That was exactly what Tracy had told her.

"I see. Well, things are different now, aren't they?"

For the first time, his eyes seemed to be troubled. "I don't know. Guess the answer lies with my question."

His question? "Which is?"

Joe took a deep breath. "I need the truth. I know you still love that man. What happened between you?"

I can't answer that. Too painful. "Let's just say, uh, he did something I can't forgive."

Joe sat back and sipped his drink through a straw. "If things between us ever progress, I expect, and will certainly give you in return, utmost honesty." He reached for her hand. "I love you, Tara, but more than that, I want you to be happy. Did the kiss I gave you the last day in the office have anything to do with you breaking up with him?"

Tara wriggled in her chair and looked everywhere but at his face. "Can we talk about something else?"

"Yes, gladly. As soon as you answer truthfully. Did it?"

Tara searched her mind. She'd been so mad at Edmund. But when she talked to Ashley afterward, she realized Edmund had tried hard, very hard, not to fall from the pedestal she had him on. Was what he'd felt any different than the attraction she had for Joe? And if she hadn't had the feelings for Joe in her back pocket, would she have reacted differently? "Yes, it did."

Joe smiled at her. "Thought so. Tara, I want you to do something and I won't take no for an answer."

"And that is?"

"Go back to him. Pretend I don't exist and that we never happened. Figure out what's happening and either patch it up or let him go, once and for all. Since we started dating, I can feel him, even now. Like there's three of us around the table."

"But Joe, I—"

He placed a finger to her lips. "I've heard it said, if you love something, let it go. If it comes back, it was meant to be. If not, it was never yours." Joe swallowed hard and the pain in his eyes couldn't be missed. "Go to him. If you really don't love him, I'll always be here. But the most important thing to me is your happiness. That's what I want most in life."

He motioned for the waitress. "See you around." Joe paid the bill and left.

***

Ashley's eyes slowly focused. Noise blaring from the apartment next door was so loud. It matched the throbbing in her head. She'd been sick for three weeks now. The last food in the apartment, crackers, had come back up right after she ate them. How many days ago was that?

Her shaking hands were empty. In desperation, Ashley searched beneath the covers until she found it. The teapot cover Harry had worn when he showed her his flowers. Back when the world was right, when he loved her. She breathed deeply, catching a faint scent of him, despite the moldy odor that now permeated through it. Caused by the wetness of constant tears.

Something hard was against her back. She pulled it out. The book Harry had written for her, 'Prayers Do Get Answered'. *Please, God. Answer my prayers. Bring Harry back to me.* The pages were worn from constant reading.

She needed help. Ashley had no idea where her phone was, as if that would help. Before the device quit working, she'd called Harry dozens of times every day, but it always went to voicemail. It didn't matter because the cell service would no longer allow messages. His mailbox was full.

A small voice within her nagged: *Call him one last time. He'll answer.*

The noise from her neighbor's wall echoed against hers. They were at it again, fighting. *Gotta get help.* But how? Wait, wasn't there a phone booth just down the street? *Make it there. He'll answer. He's waiting.*

It took nearly all of her remaining energy to find her shoes and jacket. Ashley slipped the purse over her shoulder, then grasped Harry's teapot cover and book in her hand. The trip down the four flights of stairs seemed to take days. When she opened the door to the street, it was dark. *Was the booth to the right or the left?* She couldn't remember. *Mom always said to follow the right path.* She turned to the right. Before she'd gone barely a block, the world was spinning. *So tired. Need a short nap.* Ashley fell to the sidewalk and closed her eyes. The last thing she heard was a police siren in the distance.

A hand was on her shoulder. Someone was shaking her. A man stood above her. As her eyes focused, it could be seen he wasn't alone.

The man knelt next to her. "What's wrong with you, girl? You high?"

"N-n-no. I just got tired and had to rest."

"You got tired?" another one asked. "Why you so tired?" Several of them laughed, making dirty comments. She ignored them.

"I need to get to a phone. I'm sick."

The man kneeling next to her looked concerned. "Sick? What's wrong?"

"I'm so light-headed." She realized another man was going through her purse. Ashley begged. "That's mine. Give it back!"

"What kind of drugs you been usin'? They in here?" He pulled out her wallet. "Lookie what we got here." He whistled as he removed all of Ashley's money from her wallet, stuffing it in his pocket. "That's a lot of cash. I'll take it to keep it safe for you. Won't be needin' that money tonight."

The kind man argued. "Stop it. Put her money back."

The first one continued to riffle through her wallet. "Only one credit card." He pocketed that, too. "A medical emergency card. So, you're Ashley L. Snyder from... hey guys, look at this. She's from Intercourse, Pennsylvania. You Amish, girl?"

Ashley tried to get up. "Give me back my things before I call the police."

All of them laughed. The man who had taken her money yanked Ashley to her feet, drawing her face close to his. His bad breath started to make her sicker. "That's funny. Police don't come 'round here after dark. You ain't in Intercourse no more. Gimme that ring off your finger and we'll leave you be." Ashley tried to get away, but he wouldn't let her escape. "I want that ring." He grasped hold of it.

Ashley wrapped her hands around it and screamed as loud as she could. "No. Help!"

As they struggled, a Jeep skidded to a stop along the curb near them. The window rolled down and a voice with a thick Canadian accent yelled, "Hey, leave the girl be."

Ashley's attacker shot him the finger. "Keep movin', cowboy, before I whup you and take your fancy car."

"I said you be leaving the girl alone, now, eh?"

"Find your own. This girl's mine."

The driver closed the car window and turned the engine off. The large man extricated his gigantic frame before swiftly walking around to the sidewalk. Ashley's attacker released her. She fell and the thief backed away. The giant scanned the group menacingly before kneeling next to Ashley. "You all right, ma'am?"

Ashley's head was spinning. All she could do was shake her head. The one who tried to steal her ring now attempted to shove the big man, but the newcomer didn't budge. Without taking his attention from Ashley, he gave the smaller man a thrust that sent him head over heels back onto the dirty ground. Without even a grunt, he effortlessly picked Ashley up in his arms, carrying her to his Jeep. As the giant worked on sitting her inside, Ashley's attacker hit him in the head. Without looking back, her rescuer delivered a well-placed kick to the knee, which caused the smaller man to writhe on the ground in pain. The man with the Canadian accent strapped Ashley in the car and dropped his keys in her lap. He locked the door and turned to face the gang.

Ashley stared out the window. By now, the whole group surrounded him. The big man stared at them. "Had a bad day on the ice, boys. Lost a fight and got kicked out of the game for it. You boys want to tussle with old Mick, eh? Good. I'm in the mood to fight."

The man who had tried to steal Ashley's ring took a step toward her rescuer. "We want the girl and we want her right now."

The man called Mick laughed. "Not happening, Tinkerbell. You want her, eh? Get past me. Dare ya."

One of the men tried to get to Mick's left, obviously to flank him. Without flinching or taking his eyes off the leader, his large left fist flew out and delivered a devastating blow, removing that man from action.

The gang faltered. The big man lunged at them. They ran off into the night.

With no one in sight, he grabbed her things and returned to the passenger door to check on Ashley. She was afraid she would pass out. His voice calmed her. "Mind letting me in my car?" She nodded, hitting the power lock to open the door. He climbed in the driver's seat. "You all right, miss?"

Her voice was trembling. "N-no. I n-need to find a phone. I need Harry."

"That be all? Use my phone."

Her eyes couldn't focus on the numbers. "Can you dial for me?"

"Be glad to. What's the number?"

It took her a few attempts to try and get it out. She was so exhausted. Her eyes fluttered and the world went dark.

Chapter 22

usk was overtaking daylight as Harry drove across the Susquehanna River from York into Lancaster County. Low clouds obscured the view of the beautiful state road bridge to his right. The lights from the Art Deco roadway were blurry as they struggled against the river fog. Snow covered Chickies Rock to his left and still lay heavily on the roofline of many of Columbia's buildings.

Harry wound down the window, breathing in the earthy scent of Lancaster County. Odors from a dairy farm greeted him. But not even the familiar scents or sights of this once beloved area raised his spirit. He needed to leave for his new job tomorrow night and there was much to do before then.

He yearned to see his family, but he had a stop to make first. Harry parked and walked until he stood at Mrs. Snyder's door. The memory of an evening long ago nibbled at his emotions. A time when Ashley opened the door and kissed his cheek. Harry wiped the sadness away.

The portal swung open and Harry almost recoiled at the sight. Jessica Snyder appeared to have aged thirty years since he'd last seen her.

"May I come in?"

The fire in her eyes answered his question before her words. "You are not welcome here, ever. Get off my property now or I'll call the police."

Harry took two steps back. "I know you'll never forgive me, but…"

"Forgive you? Are you crazy? You broke my little girl's heart. You once told me Ashley would always get respect from you. You fooled both of us, you liar. God might forgive you, but I never will." Mrs. Snyder slammed the door in his face.

Harry climbed back in his truck. *That went well.*

Harry stopped his truck far enough away from Henry's house to see the lights. He didn't want to talk to anyone tonight. *Nor do they want to talk to me.*

He waited thirty minutes after the last light was extinguished before pulling up, headlights off. He still had a house key, so he unlocked the door. The flickering of the fireplace from the family room caught his attention.

The smells of home and the memories of happy times flooded back. He pawed at his eyes. In less than twenty-four hours, he'd leave this place, never to return.

Harry was headed to his room when a voice called out, "Hello, Harry. Been waiting for you."

Harry spun around to see Edmund emerge from the shadows.

Edmund stood before him. His eyes were sunken and he looked horrible. "Glad you're finally here. Let's get this over with now, while everyone is sleeping."

The fire reflected an orange hue off his bandage. "Get what over with?"

Edmund drew a ragged breath. "You swore next time you saw me, you'd kill me. Put me out of my misery, please. You've every right. But before you do, I need to say something." The younger man stepped closer. "I was in love with Ashley. How could I not be? But she was yours and I tried so hard not to let it show. What happened was my fault, not hers. Forgive her. Take it all out on me. I led her astray."

Harry's hands trembled. "Edmund..."

Edmund looked down and shook his head. "I'm sorry, Harry. Do it. I don't want to live anymore."

Harry lunged forward. Edmund's eyes closed tightly until Harry hugged him. "Forgive me, Edmund. I'm sorry for hurting you. I should have let you explain."

After Edmund's initial shock wore off, the two brothers talked until the wee hours. Harry kissed his younger brother's forehead before walking to the room that had once been his. Slowly, he pushed open the door.

All of Ashley's pictures had been reframed. A pot of gladiolas welcomed him. His books were stacked neatly in the trunk. He opened the top one. Someone had painstakingly taped the pages back together. His cell phone was sitting on the edge of his dresser, charging cord attached. Harry touched the home button. Before the screen display could come on, it rang.

What? He pulled the cord from it and answered. "Hello?" In shock, he quickly responded. "Yes, I know Ashley Snyder."

***

The ticking of the kitchen clock echoed throughout the whole house. Harry's sudden appearance last night had startled Jessica. No sleep tonight. Her mind drifted back to New Year's Day. And the bad argument they'd had. All her little girl had done since the day Harry left was sit in her room and bawl. Jessica had enough of it.

"Ashley, stop this. It's time to get over Harry."

"I can't, Mom. I love him. Can't you understand that?"

She had smoothed her daughter's hair. *"I know you do, but he obviously doesn't love you. If he did, he wouldn't have treated you like he did. Thank God Ellie was there to save you."*

"No, no. It wasn't like that at all. He was just, just upset over what I did. It's all my fault."

She had shaken her daughter. *"Stop it! You weren't responsible. He's no good. Fooled both of us. It's time to forget him and move on."*

"Mom, I can't. He'll come back. I know he will. I love him and I know he loves me."

"Quit saying things that aren't true. It was all infatuation. He just happened to be the first man to pay any attention to you, that's all."

Ashley had shaken her head. *"That's not true. He loved me. Still does. Harry will come back. As sure as God's in heaven, I know he will. Wait and see."*

"And if he does, I'll have the police arrest him for trespassing. I'm surprised they didn't arrest him already for assaulting his brother."

"He was just angry at Edmund."

"Bull crap! He's a monster. I'm glad this came out before you married him and he ended up abusing you. If I ever see his face again, it'll be too soon. Now, I forbid you to think about him or mention his name again."

"I'm nineteen. You can't boss me around."

"As long as you live under my roof, you'll do as I tell you. If you're that blind and too stupid to realize he was only using you, there's something wrong with you. Go to your room and don't come out until you get some common sense."

Ashley stormed from the room. The last time she'd seen her little girl. Ashley left home while Jessica was at work the next day. *Where are you, Ashley? God, please bring her back to me.*

A pounding noise shook the whole house, like a giant woodpecker was hammering against the walls. Jessica Snyder quickly sat up. *What in the world?* A man's voice rang out. It was him. That no good Harry Campbell.

"Mrs. Snyder. Come to the door, quickly. It's an emergency!"

Throwing a housecoat around her shoulders, she stumbled to the front door and flicked on the porch light. Yep, the idiot was standing there, all right. She kept the door between them locked. Her cell was in her hand. She punched in '911'. If he threatened her or didn't leave, she'd hit the send button.

Through the closed door Jessica hollered, "Why are you here? Do you know what time of day it is? Thought I told you to get off my property. Should I call the police?"

"No, wait. I got a call *about* Ashley."

Her whole body trembled. *Call* about *Ashley?* Jessica dropped her phone into her pocket. "What? Is she okay?"

Harry was shaking his head. "A man called. Said he found Ashley on the street. She'd been robbed. She's sick, but refused to go to the hospital."

Jessica threw open the door. "Robbed? Where is she?"

"Philadelphia. I'm heading there now. Come with me. Ashley needs us."

"Us? You turned your back on her. Stay away from my daughter."

"No. Leaving her was the stupidest thing I ever did. I'll never make that mistake again. You coming with me or not?"

"How do I know this isn't some game you're playing?"

He stood tall before her, fire in his eyes. "I'll never play games when it comes to Ashley. He said she asked for me. I'm leaving now. Want to come or not?"

Jessica hesitated.

Harry's face turned red. "Fine. I'll go by myself." He turned and ran to the car.

Ashley. Robbed? *My poor baby.* He won't know what to do. Jessica called after him. "Wait. Let me get dressed."

Within ten minutes, they were flying down the Lincoln Highway.

Jessica listened as Harry explained some man had called less than an hour ago. The voice told Harry he'd come to Ashley's aid during a robbery. Ashley had told the unknown man to call Harry. He'd provided the name of the hotel and said he'd wait with her until Harry arrived.

"Are you sure this isn't a prank? Do you even know if he's with Ashley?"

"Oh, yes. He's with her. Bet my life on it."

"How can you be so sure?"

"She wouldn't let go of something in her hand. When he described it, I knew he was telling the truth."

"What was it?"

Harry had to control his voice before answering, "A teapot cover."

It was Ashley! She hadn't let that stupid cover out of her hands the entire time after he'd left. Jessica looked at the speedometer. Eighty-five miles an hour. "Is this all the faster you can go?"

Daylight was starting to fight off the clouds when Harry pulled into the motel lot. He slammed the gearshift into park. "Said they're in room 236."

Jessica had to run to keep up with Harry as he took the stairs to the second floor two at a time. He barreled down the hall until he stood in front of the door.

Harry knocked. A tall and large man opened it. "Who be you?"

"Harry Campbell. Where's Ashley?"

The man pulled the door open. "In the bed." Harry brushed past him, Jessica trailing by mere inches.

Ashley looked horrible. Her eyes were puffy and she was pale. She'd lost weight, a lot of weight. Harry dropped to his knees and kissed her forehead. His voice was soft. "Princess? I'm here. So's your mom." He gently shook Ashley's arm. "Princess?"

Ashley's eyes slowly opened. Bloodshot. Tired. A worried look covered her face. "Harry? Is that really you, or am I dreaming again?"

Harry cupped her face. "It's me, princess, really me."

Ashley drew a ragged breath, but a smile grew. "I knew you'd come, you old pot head." With trembling arms, she reached for Harry. "I love you. Knew you'd come find me."

Harry was trying to maintain his composure, but failed. His voice was high when he replied, "I love you, too, princess. Please forgive me."

"Nothing to forgive."

***

While Jessica helped Ashley to the bathroom, Harry turned to the giant. "You look very familiar. Have we met before?"

His smile revealed two missing front teeth. "No, but you've probably seen me at a game. Name's Mickey. Mickey Campeau."

Harry did a double take. "The hockey player?"

"Yep. That be me. Good thing I came along for your girl there. Bunch of hoodlums were roughing her up. She said they cleaned out her wallet. Tried to take that ring off her hand, but she got spunk, you know?"

Harry could feel his jaw clench. *Calm down. You swore to God never to lose your temper again.* "Thank you for helping Ashley."

Mickey slapped his shoulder. "That ring came from you, eh?"

"Yes, sir."

"Sir? That be my dad. No need to call me that. Your girl kept talkin' about you comin' to get her. I think you be a lucky man, eh?"

Harry forced his shoulders to relax. "I hope so. If she'll forgive me."

Mickey laughed. "Don't know what you did, but I believe you be forgiven already. Saw her eyes light up when you woke her."

Harry could feel his cheeks warm. "Let me give you money for the room."

"That be nice, but no. You'da done the same thing if that'd been my sister on the street."

"I'd like to think so."

Jessica helped Ashley back into the room. Ashley reached for Harry and latched onto him. "I missed you so much."

Mickey grabbed his coat. "That be my cue to leave. Nice to have met you folks." He turned to Ashley. "And you, miss. Seems your prince charming be here."

Ashley seemed ready to fall over, but she shook her head. Harry scooped her in his arms.

Ashley had trouble getting the words out. "He's a king, not a prince. My king. King Harry."

Mickey doubled over with laughter. "In the presence of royalty, am I? Well, you two go off an' live a fairy tale, eh?"

Mrs. Snyder seemed awestruck. "Wait! You, you're Mickey, uh. That hockey player, aren't you?"

He shot her a smile, displaying the gap between his canines again. "Dat be me. Really gotta go."

Harry took a step toward him, Ashley in his arms. "How can we ever repay your kindness?"

"You got my number. Invite me to the wedding. Ain't never been to a royal wedding, eh? It be fun. Bye now." He quickly left the room.

Ashley clung even tighter against Harry. "Did you come back to stay?"

Harry kissed her hair. "Until the day I die, ever and forever."

***

Edmund dragged himself into the house, breathing in the luscious scent of his mother's freshly baked bread. But the aroma didn't even appeal to him anymore. It had been a long, hard day spent repairing the watering system in one of the hot houses. His arm ached, but not as much as his heart. He missed Tara. Edmund had tried to talk to her, but she refused to even listen.

Henry greeted him. "Did you hear the news?"

The obvious joy in his brother's face piqued interest. "What's that?"

"Harry and Jessica found Ashley. She spent the day in the hospital, but she's coming home tonight."

"Did she and Harry..."

Henry was as giddy as a schoolboy at holiday. "Yes, yes. They worked out their problems. We're all going over to visit tonight. Want to come along?"

Edmund was happy for Harry, but he couldn't face Ashley. Not after what he'd done or the hurt he'd caused not only Ashley, but Harry as well. *Not to mention hurting Tara and destroying my future.* "I, uh, don't..."

"Maybe Edmund could stay here tonight and watch Maggie." Edmund turned to find Ellie standing there, holding her little girl. It was easy to see the compassion on her face. *Wonderful Ellie.* So kind. So special. Just like his Tara.

"If my brother doesn't mind, that would be great."

This was his out. "Don't mind at all."

As the family ate dinner, the talk was all about Harry and Ashley. But Edmund's mind was somewhere else. On his past – the girl living down the road as well as his bleak future in the land three thousand miles east. This place would never be home anymore, not without Tara. He'd made the decision to return to beloved Scotland.

Everyone departed around six. Edmund played with little Maggie, wondering if she'd miss him when he was gone. Like she'd obviously missed Harry. Every time the door opened, her head had turned, looking for Uncle Harry.

Ellie had given Maggie a bath, so after changing her, Edmund dressed his niece in the Minnie Mouse nightgown her mother had laid out. The pair snuggled in the rocker. Edmund opened one of the storybooks Harry had written. The pages were taped together. Something Edmund had painstakingly done with all of the torn books. A tribute to the brother he thought he'd lost forever.

Maggie sucked her thumb as she wriggled deep into his arms.

Never have children of my own. "Uncle Edmund will be going away soon. Might be the last time I get to read to you." The baby's eyes were focused on the dancing flames. His were blurry. "This book is titled *'Frederick the Fox'*. Written by your Uncle Harry." Maggie was asleep before page three. Edmund finished the book and took her to Henry's room. He turned on the monitor, returned to the kitchen and brewed a cup of tea.

Tara's scent filled the room, like it always did when he thought of her. He was sitting in the rocker, staring at the fireplace when he heard a noise behind him. Edmund glanced over his shoulder and almost dropped his cup when he saw her standing there. "Tara?"

She nodded and sat in the other rocker.

Edmund's heart was beating loudly in his ears. "How long have you been here?"

"Long enough to hear you tell Maggie you're leaving. When are you going?"

"Soon, I don't know yet."

Tara's voice was soft. "Why?"

She wasn't looking at him, but he couldn't take his eyes off her. "I screwed up everything. I can't stay here, this close to you, knowing I ruined us. It's killing me."

"I can't stand you living here, either. Next to me, yet so far away."

"I'm sorry. I'll be gone soon."

Tara blew her nose. "Why didn't you visit Ashley, like everyone else?"

He gulped hard. "After what I did? I can't face her."

Tara turned to him. "Did you really love her?"

Edmund dropped his eyes. "No. Yes. Maybe. Makes no difference. Shouldn't have said anything or kissed her. I want you to know, even though I might have loved her, I loved you more. And our love was deep and real."

Tara sat back in the rocker, eyes closed. "I understand. I found someone else. Dr. Joseph Rohrer. Such a kind man." Her lips curled into a smile. "The perfect man. I fell in love with him."

Despite knowing they were over, hearing these words from her lips broke his heart in two. He had to bite his lips, hard. "I'm happy for you. Hope he's everything you ever want."

She studied the fire for a few moments before speaking again. "There's only one problem with Joe."

Edmund turned to see her face. "What problem?"

Tara turned toward him. Her cheeks were wet. "He's not you." She stood and walked to him.

Edmund got out of the chair to face her. "I'm sorry."

"My heart will never be whole. Not without you." Tara touched his cheek and kissed his lips, so softly.

He couldn't help himself. He wrapped his arms around Tara.

She pulled away. "Don't leave. Let's work this out."

Edmund's arms fell and he took a step backwards. "What? I think I heard you wrong."

"No, you didn't. Let's reset the clock, to before this happened. I understand how you felt, now. Can we pick up where we left off?"

He was shaking so badly. "I want that more than anything."

"Then kiss me."

She didn't have to ask a second time.

Epilogue

*H*enry sealed the last envelope and threw it on the stack of mail. *I hate paperwork.* Maybe it was time to listen to Ellie and hire a full time business manager. The photo on his desk drew his attention. Henry picked it up, smiling at the image. All three brothers, and their brides.

Henry's arm was throbbing tonight. As he rubbed it, he shook his head in disbelief. For years his brothers had disagreed about everything. Yet beyond belief, they'd decided to get married, the same day, in a dual ceremony with Henry as their best man. In the photo, both brothers were sporting their red tartan kilts as they stood next to their brides.

Tara was laughing, as if to say 'the joke's on you, Edmund'. Married only two months before, she was pregnant already. Edmund was going to be a father and couldn't be prouder. Or happier. Henry couldn't believe the difference a year had made. Then, Edmund had distanced from the family by his own choice. And now? Edmund had taken much of the workload from Henry by managing the hot houses.

And there stood Harry and Ashley. Which had the bigger or goofier smile? That was impossible to tell. And of course they were wearing those ridiculous teapot covers on their heads in the photo, as they had for the wedding. At Ashley's encouragement, Harry now worked on his books full time. One of these days, he'd make the right connection and his new career would take off. In the meanwhile, Ashley supported them by managing the Tea Room in Sophie's absence. Jessica Snyder had quit her old job and worked for her daughter as the Tea Room hostess. Of course, they took off when Mickey Campeau's team was playing home games. He'd given the three of them season tickets. Mickey was a frequent visitor in the Tea Room and had become good friends with Mrs. Snyder. He was active in the cancer charity efforts of both women.

But the girl with the biggest smile was Ellie, his own wife. She wore a white dress with yellow flowers, a close replica of the one she'd worn on the day he'd proposed. So wonderful. Still the most beautiful girl he'd ever seen.

Henry laughed when he saw his own image standing there next to Ellie. He was dressed in his Royal Marine uniform, wearing the Green Beret he'd earned for passing Commando training. Since he was the best man, Ellie had given him a choice. Henry could wear a kilt or his dark blue parade dress uniform. He was proud (and relieved) that his Royal Marine uniform still fit without alteration.

The ringing of his cell broke the mental trip down memory lane. He smiled when he saw the caller ID. Ellie was on FaceTime.

"Henry, how's my husband? I felt you thinking about me."

"Of course I was thinking about you, Ellie. Looking at the wedding photo on my desk and thinking of my soulmate... the best thing to ever happen to me. How are you and Maggie doing down there in Savannah with your family?"

"Missing you. She's here with me, trying to grab the phone. Want to say hello?"

Henry spoke to his daughter for a few minutes before Ellie came back on. Those brown eyes were so pretty.

"Don't forget, Ben drove to New York today. I want you to spend the night at their house. Sophie shouldn't be alone, this close to her due date." Henry smiled but didn't say anything. "What?"

"You, Ellie. You're something else. Most women wouldn't ask their husbands to stay with another woman while they're out of town."

Ellie's smile brought out her dimples. "Most women don't have the close relationship with their husbands like you and I share."

Henry laughed. "What you mean is I couldn't get away with anything because you'd feel it."

Ellie shot him a wink. "That's true, but you forget. I know how much you love me."

"Yes, I do. As soon as Ben gets back, I'll be on my way to be with you."

"I can't wait. Oh, by the way, I've got a secret to tell you."

"What is it?"

"If I told you, it wouldn't be a secret. I'll wait until we're together."

"Hmm. Maybe I'll read your mind."

Ellie's lips filled the screen. "Let me tell you in person. I've got to get going. Tell Sophie I said hello. And Henry? I love you."

***

Henry walked the short distance to the Miller's. Sophie was seated on the swing out front, wearing a blue sleeveless maternity top and shorts. Lately, she appeared to be exhausted. Today was no different, but she sported that wonderful smile she always had for him. Sophie offered a glass of iced tea, then reached up to lightly kiss his cheek.

"How are you feeling today, Sophie?"

"Pretty tired. Little Isaiah is kicking his mother unmercifully. He wants out. Like to feel him?" Henry nodded and she reached for his hand, pulling up her top so his hand was on her bare stomach. As good as his mother's word, her son kicked at Henry's touch.

"Does seem to be a lively chap, doesn't he?"

"I hope he turns out to be the type of man his real father is."

Henry frowned and shook his head. "We've talked about this before. Ben's his real father."

She gave him a tired smile. "I know, but if it hadn't been for you, I wouldn't be pregnant."

"You two would have found a suitable donor."

"Maybe, but my best friend fathered my child. Thank you. I hope you know how much I love you."

He took her hand. "I love you, too, Sophie. Please don't say things like that anymore. I don't want you to offend Ben."

It was her turn to frown. "Pretty hot out here. Help me into the house where it's cooler."

Henry noticed Sophie was walking a little different. He helped her to the sofa, watching her grimace with pain. "What do you want to eat?"

"A roast beef sandwich and watermelon. Stuff's in the fridge, but I don't have the energy to make it."

As he prepared their food, they talked about their days. Something was different about Sophie. Henry noted she only pushed her food around on her plate. "Everything all right, Soph?"

She nodded, not even glancing at him. "Just down in the dumps a little. I don't think Isaiah likes his mummy today. Treating me horridly."

"What can I do to help?"

She turned to him. "Can we have a serious conversation?"

"Of course. What would you like to talk about?"

A tingling sensation ran up his spine when she answered, "Us."

"Us? What do you mean, our friendship?"

Her cheeks turned red. "Do you know how much I love you?"

"I love you, too. Next to Ellie, you're my best friend."

"And if that isn't enough for me? Suppose I need more? Are you willing to love me more?"

Please no. "I don't understand the question. I love you as a friend. Only as a friend."

"Henry, I want more than being friends."

He stared into her eyes for a long time. "Sophia, I love Ellie. If you're asking for a romantic relationship or even an affair, the answer's no. My heart belongs to Ellie and always will."

"You misunderstand me. It has nothing to do with romance, but just being best friends isn't enough for me. And never call me Sophia, I always want to be Sophie to you."

Henry shivered. "I'm not sure what you want. Are you and Benjy having problems?"

Sophie struggled to find a comfortable position. "What do you remember about the day we met? What did you think of me?"

Henry chewed on his lip. "I thought you were quite beautiful, but there was a sadness about you. My heart went out to you."

She nodded. "I hated my life, the loneliness, the heartlessness of my supposed friends. I was so depressed." Sophie was staring at a spot on the wall. "The day we met was going to be my last. I'd decided to end it all that night."

A wave of cold rolled over Henry. "What?"

"There was no good in my life. I wanted it to be over. Then you showed up, offering a glimmer of hope. I postponed my death one day, then a second, then indefinitely. You are my rock, the reason I'm alive. That's why I love you so much. You saved my life."

"Sophie, I never had a clue."

"Henry, you know me better than anyone, my parents, Benjy or Ellie. Since we met, you've always been there for me. I don't know why, but lately, I'm scared we'll drift apart. If Ben stopped loving me, somehow I'd survive. But losing you? That would kill me."

"Sophie, I'm not going away."

"Good, but promise me you'll always be my closest friend. No, the word *friend* doesn't even come close. I need to know that when I get old and fat, when my hair turns gray, when I'm unlovable, you'll still be there, forever. When we both die and go to Heaven, I want to know you'll be there with me."

"Sophie, I will. Our friendship is based on mutual trust, on mutual, oh I don't know the word..."

Sophie rubbed her stomach. "On mutual love. Promise me you'll be more than just my best friend, promise me you will be my eternal friend. I can't put it into words, but you mean the world to me."

He offered his hand and she grasped it, tightly. "I promise you, Sophie, I'll always be there. Do you believe me?"

She sadly smiled. "There was a reason God brought you into my life. Sometimes, I wonder what it would have been like, if you and I got together."

Not going down that path. "I refuse to even talk about that. I love Ellie and you love Ben."

Sophie nodded and looked away. "You're right. Thank you, Henry, for giving in to the wishes of a tired, emotional, pregnant woman. I feel the need to rest. I need my eternal friend to be with me for a while. Could you hold my hand until I fall asleep?" Henry offered his hand, which Sophie took. She quickly dozed off.

Henry didn't turn on the TV. Instead, he watched Sophie sleep. She'd been right. God had brought them together for a purpose. He finally understood why he was so important to her. His mind replayed their past. The years of friendship, holidays spent together. Sophie had been his rock when Ellie had been kidnapped. Her strength bolstered him when everyone said Ellie was dead. Yes, God had brought them together, because He knew they needed each other.

Sophie moaned and tried to re-position herself.

Henry knelt next to her. "Are you all right?"

"I can't get comfortable. My son's taking his frustrations out on me. Mind talking to me for a little while, until I fall back to sleep? Your voice is so comforting."

"What do you want to talk about?"

"Tell me the story of us, of our friendship. Such a lovely story." Sophie reached for his hand. Within five minutes, she was loudly snoring. The sofa was not very comfortable, but Henry managed to fall asleep.

Around midnight, Sophie cried out. Henry woke immediately.

"Sophie, what's wrong?"

Her voice was tear stained. "It hurts, Henry. Please help me."

"Are you having contractions?"

"I thought Isaiah was just kicking mummy, but maybe these are contractions. Please call the doctor."

The doctor told him to get her to the hospital immediately. In less than fifteen minutes, he had her in the car, along with her pre-packed suitcase. Henry used the hands-free setting to call Ellie.

Despite the early hour, Ellie answered immediately. "Henry? What's wrong? I can feel your anxiety."

Sophie cried out from a contraction. "I'm taking Sophie to the hospital."

"Sophie's in labor, isn't she?"

"Yes."

"Stay with her, Henry. I'll see if I can get hold of Ben. I love you. Keep me updated."

Henry made it to the hospital and helped her to the triage desk. When he returned after parking the car, the nurse told him she'd take him to maternity to be with Sophie.

"I'm not her husband. Should I still come?"

The nurse eyed him strangely. "She said she wanted the baby's father in the room with her. Are you the baby's father?"

Henry's face heated. "Yes, I am."

"Then follow me."

As soon as he entered the room, Sophie reached for Henry's hand. A doctor was examining her. "Benjy isn't here. I need you to be with me."

The doctor stood and stripped off his gloves. "You should have come in sooner, Mrs. Miller. You're almost fully dilated. We're heading to delivery, now." The doctor barked out some orders to the attending nurse. Within seconds, the bed was moving, Henry in tow. Even if Henry wanted to let go, Sophie had his hand clamped tightly in hers.

He quickly assumed the role of Sophie's coach. During contractions, Sophie gripped his hands so tightly his fingers turned white. After the latest contraction passed, Sophie collapsed on the bed.

"Please don't leave me, Henry. Need you now more than I ever did."

Henry grabbed a cloth and wiped the perspiration from her face. "I'll stay here as long as you need me. You're doing a great job." The doctor waited until she had three more contractions before doing another exam.

"Next contraction, I want you to push." It seemed only a few seconds before the pain again wracked her body. She clung to Henry as if her life depended on it.

The doctor spoke in a calm tone. "Doing good, Sophie. This is it. Push, push, *push!*" Sophie did and screamed in pain.

"The head's coming. One more push." Sophie did and Isaiah Thomas Miller entered the world. The doctor held the baby by his feet and smacked his behind. The baby cried. So did Sophie. Henry held her tightly.

As soon as they cut the cord and cleaned him up, the nurse handed the infant to his mother. She cried as she held him. "Henry, come see our son."

Henry looked at the child. "He's your son, Sophie. Yours and Ben's, not mine. I'm gonna call Ellie."

Sophie grabbed his hand. "Henry, thank you. I'm so thankful God brought you into my life. We're friends, eternal friends, forever. I love you."

He briefly brushed his lips to her forehead. "Love you, too, Soph."

Suddenly, Sophie drew a sharp breath. Henry followed her eyes to the man in the doorway, her husband Ben. Sophie's husband had a sad look on his face, but smiled when he caught his wife's gaze.

Sophie's voice was cracking as she exclaimed, "Oh Benjy, come look at your boy."

Ben took the infant from his mother and examined him from head to toe. "Soph, he's perfect, just like his mother." Ben leaned down to kiss his wife. "Thank you for making my dreams come true. I love you so much."

Warm feelings filled Henry's chest. Seeing his best friends basking in happiness made him long for his wife and daughter. Now that Benjamin was back home with Sophie, he was free to head south to join his girls.

"I'm going to say goodbye, now. I need to touch base with Edmund on a few things before I leave. I'm so happy for you."

Ben still held his son, but he squeezed Henry's shoulder. "I don't have words to say how grateful I am. Thanks, Henry."

"Glad I could be of assistance." He turned to Sophie. Her arms were opened wide to hold him.

Henry stepped into her embrace. Her breath was warm against his ear. "Thank you, Henry. I love you, but you know that." She grabbed his head and captured his eyes. "I have one favor to ask before you go."

"What can I do for you?"

Sophie swallowed hard and her eyes widened. "It's not for me, but for Isaiah."

Her expression made him laugh. Sophie joined him. "What does little Isaiah want?"

Sophie looked at Ben. Henry caught his nod. "Isaiah needs a little sister to play with."

***

As soon as his flight landed, Henry could sense Ellie. He rushed through the airport, leaving the secured area quickly. He searched for Ellie, but her squeal indicated she saw him first. Henry swept her into his arms. Ellie's lips tasted like honey. The kiss was long, because neither could get enough of the other. Eventually, they made it to her car.

When they arrived at the big rambling house where her parents lived, his other girl smiled when she saw him. The baby chattered at Henry, "Da-da, da-da."

Ellie's parents hosted a party in the afternoon to introduce Maggie to their friends. While both Henry and Ellie enjoyed the party, they couldn't wait to be alone. Finally, Henry closed the door to Ellie's childhood room. After Maggie May entered dreamland, at last they had a chance to hold each other.

Henry nuzzled Ellie's neck. "Ellie, I love you so much."

She kissed her husband deeply and then pulled away. "I love you, too, but I'm very disappointed in you."

Henry sat up in the bed so he could see her face more clearly. "What did I do? Tell me so I can correct it."

Ellie giggled. "Henry, can't you read my mind? Aren't you the least bit interested in my secret?"

"I forgot all about it. Tell me, what's your secret?"

Her smile was enchanting as she whispered, "You're gonna be a daddy again."

A fearful nagging feeling crawled up his spine. *Sophie did it again!* She'd obviously told Ellie. "W-w-what do you m-m-mean?"

Ellie's smile couldn't be any larger. "I'm pregnant. Hope we have a son this time!"

Henry let out a sigh of relief as his heart leapt for joy. "Oh, Ellie. I'm so happy. So in love with you."

She kissed him again. "I love you, forever." They fell asleep in each other's arms, dreaming about their love, their future, their lives. It didn't matter that they were in Savannah. As long as they were together, they were in paradise.

The End

Other Things You Should Know...

Twelve years ago, freshmen Eleanor Lucia and Benjamin Miller met at college. They quickly fell in love, but their romance ended shortly after graduation.

Ten years ago, Henry Campbell mustered out of the Royal Marines. He took a job at a travel agency and met Sophia Sarduci. While not romantic, a deep relationship developed between them.

Six years ago, Kaitlin and Jeremy Roberts took their niece Eleanor Lucia into their care after a bout of severe depression and alcoholism. Ellie's parents had turned their backs on her. Kaitlin and Jeremy helped Ellie recover and rebuild her life. They love and care for Ellie as if she were their daughter.

Four years ago, Eleanor Lucia disappeared just before her wedding to Henry Campbell. Based on the brutal crime scene and evidence, the police declared Eleanor dead. Henry refused to believe it. He and his sister Margaret searched for Eleanor, discovered where she was being held and rescued her. Henry nearly died during the rescue.

Three and a half years ago, Eleanor Lucia and Henry Campbell wed and moved next to their best friends, Benjamin and Sophia Miller. Six months later, Henry and Margaret Campbell found Campbell Farms. Henry moved his two younger brothers and mother to live with them in Paradise, Pennsylvania.

Other Books by this Author

Seeking Forever (Book 1)

Kaitlin Jenkins is selected to embark on a six-month work project, out of her comfort zone and far away from her support network. If only she hadn't been assigned such a distractingly handsome partner—a former Army Ranger.

Jeremy is making his first foray into the civilian world. But he was not prepared to spend half a year on the road with a woman who seems even more heartless than his ex-wife.

Can love overcome the misunderstandings between them and the challenges of life on the road?

Seeking Happiness (Book 2)

Kelly lives a happy life. A great marriage, four wonderful kids and a fulfilling job managing an emergency department in L.A. But the day after her sister's wedding, her husband breaks the news. He is leaving her for Hollywood's hottest young actress and Kelly's world crumbles.

Then she meets the man of her dreams – smart, cute and romantic. The love of her life. And that's when the trouble really begins. Will she fill the hole in her heart? Will she ever find happiness and love again?

Seeking Eternity (Book 3)

One bright September day long ago, Stanley Jenkins told his best friend, "See that girl? I'm going to marry her someday." Stan and Nora Thomas became best friends – soulmates – and fell in love. But when she told him she was engaged, he walked out of her life so she could find happiness. The loss was devastating.

Years later, when a waitress asks, "Stan, is that really you?" he looks up into the beautiful eyes of Nora, the girl he still loves. She's been widowed by her first husband, however Stan sadly notices the engagement ring on her hand. Once again, they become best friends... but as her wedding day approaches, is the cycle doomed to repeat?

Seeking the Pearl (Book 4)

Ellie Lucia is a spectator in her own life... a life of sorrow and loneliness... even while working abroad in London, until Henry Campbell sweeps her off her American feet. Suddenly the world is bright and full of promise. But just when paradise is within her grasp, she disappears. Almost everyone believes Ellie is dead. Everyone except Henry. Henry still feels Ellie in his soul. He vows to look for her until the day he dies. But will he be too late, or can true love save the day?

About the Author

Chas Williamson's lifelong dream was to write. He started writing his first book at age eight, but quit after two paragraphs. He used the gift of writing many times over the years for work and social entertainment. At the turn of the century, he wrote his first full length book, *The HazMateer,* but then 9/11 occurred and Chas decided not to pursue that genre.

It is said one should write what one knows best. That left two choices – the world of environmental health and safety... or romance. Chas and his bride have built a life of romance over the years. At her encouragement, he began writing romance. The characters you'll meet in his books are very real to him, like real life friends, He hopes they become just as real to you.

Made in the USA
Middletown, DE
24 March 2019